# THE GREAT
## CONDOMINIUM
### REBELLION

# THE GREAT CONDOMINIUM REBELLION

## CAROL SNYDER

### ILLUSTRATED BY ANTHONY KRAMER

A YEARLING BOOK

Published by
Dell Publishing Co., Inc.
1 Dag Hammarskjold Plaza
New York, New York 10017

For information address
Delacorte Press, New York, New York

Yearling ® TM 913705, Dell Publishing Co., Inc.

ISBN: 0-440-43123-9

Reprinted by arrangement with Delacorte Press
Printed in the United States of America
First Yearling printing—June 1983

CW

*With love to Regina and Joe Rich,*
*Florida's good guys.*
*With appreciation to my Florida Research*
*team of volunteers,*
*and with special thanks to Judy Blume*
*for her encouragement and friendship.*

# 1
# EXPECTATIONS

---

Dear Stacy & Marc,

Here are seven stamped postcards for the nine days you'll be in Florida. Please scribble a line or two and send a card home each day there's a mail delivery so we'll know you're alive. Have fun. Be good.

Love,
Mom (& Dad)

---

I put the postcards and Mom's note back into my jeans pocket, crumpling the recipe for chicken with almonds I'd clipped from the newspaper to give to Grandma. My mom calls me the Mad Clipper, and my dad insists on reading all newspapers before I get my hands on them.

I pressed my face against the tiny airplane window. Stars were sparkling and the whirring noise of the engines made my braces vibrate and my nose itch. My lemon-shampooed hair and grape lip gloss made

1

me smell like fruit punch. (I've always been very sensitive to smells.)

Marc cracked his knuckles. I do that, too, when I'm nervous, or sort of not telling the truth. It must be a family habit. Marc and I are a lot alike. I just turned thirteen and he's a year younger, but I'm small for my age so we're both the same size. And according to our mother we're also both fresh. In fact, one of her many last instructions was "Don't talk back to Grandma and Grandpa."

I could picture our mother if our plane ever crashed. When she heard the news she'd be sorry that her *very* last words to me and Marc had been, "Stacy —did you take the rubber bands for your braces? And Marc—don't forget what a hairbrush is for." (Sometimes I imagine what things would be like if I died or if Marc died. Sometimes I even pretend my mother or father died. I'm not weird or anything. I only do it once in a while.)

As I was thinking all this Marc leaned over me to see the stars out the window. He smelled like Old Spice after-shave lotion and Juicy Fruit gum. He doesn't shave yet but he likes to smell like he does. It's like me using deodorant even though I don't need it.

I couldn't believe we were finally going to Florida. For the past month we'd been making big plans. This would be a perfect vacation, with our grandparents all to ourselves for nine days. In Brooklyn, before they sold their shoe store and retired, Grandma and Grandpa Zimmerman had always loved talking with us and telling us about how things used to be. And now it would be great in Florida. They'd take us to the beach and pool, and we'd do all kinds of things—just us together, like friends.

I was really looking forward to it. I'd worked super hard in school this past marking period. My grades went up from C's to B's, but my spirits were definitely below average. Seventh grade and the new junior high reminded me of the kaleidoscope my grandmother gave me when I was in first grade. Everything was always changing. A million teachers instead of one or two who knew me well. Kids that like you one minute and hate you the next. If you wear the wrong kind of sneakers they think you're a durf or something and you begin to believe them. I really needed this vacation. Grandparents always think you're terrific.

"I'm gonna dive into the pool first thing tomorrow morning," I said to Marc. "And I can almost taste Grandma's stewed chicken and rice with her special tomato sauce." I swallowed. My grandmother loves to cook chicken.

"And chocolate-pudding pie," Marc added, licking his lips.

"Tennis and swimming! We're gonna have a ball." I pushed the hair out of my eyes, but it's shaggy and it went right back again. Marc's hair is like that, too, and we both have blue eyes. Those things must run in our family.

"I can't wait to see the rec room," Marc added. "Grandpa's letter said it's all built, and there are pool tables and Ping-Pong tables and even an art room. We'll really be busy."

3

Marc and I get along better than most brothers and sisters, I guess. My friend Sherry told me her brother once twisted her arm so badly she had to get X rays. Marc would never do that. Push and shove, maybe, but not twist. He let me have the window seat on the plane. Of course I *did* give him half of my pack of Life Savers in exchange. And anyway last year when we all flew to Bermuda—the vacation was my dad's company bonus for selling the most computers—Marc got the window seat both ways.

Marc poked me and pointed to the FASTEN YOUR SEAT BELT sign. The plane was getting ready to land.

I tried to picture Lemon Cove. That's the name of the condominium apartment development Grandma and Grandpa Zimmerman moved into when they retired in September. (It seems like years since we saw them. They kept their promise, though. They said we could spend Christmas vacation with them. They even sent us tickets to Fort Lauderdale for our Chanukah present. This night flight was a special bargain rate.) I imagined that Lemon Cove would have rolling hills of grass. And it would have apartments surrounded by big palm trees with coconuts, and orange and lemon trees.

As the plane braked and the engines reversed, the sign blinked off and a loudspeaker crackled. The stewardess announced that our arrival time was 11:05 P.M.—ten minutes late. She thanked everyone for traveling on this plane and wished us all a Merry Christmas. It would have been nice if she'd also said "Happy Chanukah," too, since tomorrow would be the first evening of our Jewish holiday. For the next eight nights we'd light candles and celebrate the holiday with Grandma and Grandpa.

The plane was still moving, so we didn't get up yet. I started waving out the window. I couldn't see anyone but Grandma and Grandpa were probably out there somewhere. My heart was beating fast. I swallowed hard so my ears would unclog—my father had told me to do that. When the plane stopped we unbuckled and got up.

I couldn't wait to see Grandma and Grandpa and hug them, but there were a lot of people on the plane (mostly kids or old people with shopping bags— being a people watcher, I notice things like that) and we had to stand in line a long time. Thoughts about Grandma filled my mind. I could almost taste her special chocolate chocolate-chip cookies already. I remembered being little and how we'd bake together. In that big old kitchen in Brooklyn, she never cared if flour got all over the place.

"What's a little mess when you're having a good time," she'd say. In their Brooklyn house the linoleum had a long crack in one corner. Grandma had this pink step stool so she could reach the high cabinet shelves. I loved to climb on it when I was little.

I took the comb out of my pocket. For some reason my mother thinks hair should look especially neat around grandparents. I handed the comb to Marc, but he pushed it back at me. Marc and I both have shoulder-length hair and because I haven't started to develop yet, we look alike. My friends seem to be changing and growing faster than I am. Most of my friends have even liked boys already, and I don't mean just as friends. I wonder when I'll be ready to really like a boy, and how will I know? Sometimes I worry about that. I kind of like things to stay the same.

Finally the line started moving and we walked out the tunnellike walkway. Off in the distance the first thing we saw was a bunch of tan faces, some topped with berets, baseball caps, or pushed-up eyeglasses. The women were wearing print shirts and dresses or plaid pants, and a few men had on Bermuda shorts, baggy and too long—their legs seemed decorated with veins. Everyone was waving. I searched the crowd for a familiar face.

"Stacy! Stacy and Marc!" Grandma called in her special high-pitched voice, the one she uses to find us in crowds, like in Brooklyn when she used to take us to the beach at Coney Island.

"There they are," Marc shouted, giving my hand a tug. We started to run, waving at them and calling, "Here we are!"

"Don't run!" some bald man who was waiting for someone shouted to us.

Suddenly I was being smothered with wet Grandma Zimmerman kisses and her wonderful perfume smell. Grandpa hugged Marc and then me. I could feel his heart pounding. He smiled and took a long look at us.

"It's so good to see you," he said. "You look marvelous . . . but pale. We'll soon fix that."

"That's for sure," said Grandma. "You'll go back with rosy cheeks and full stomachs. We'll see to that."

6

And she kissed us again. I could see Marc had lipstick on his cheek. I probably did, too.

"You look so tan!" I said to my grandparents.

Marc didn't say anything. He was busy wiping the lipstick off.

Grandpa took our baggage checks and started to walk away, but turned around, smiled, took another long look at us, and gave us each a kiss on the forehead. "How are your mother and father? Your father sold a million computers yet, huh? Your mother likes being a working woman? Everything is all right?"

"Talk later," Grandma said. "There are crowds at the baggage counter already."

"I'll help," Marc offered.

"Me, too," I added, wishing I'd said it first.

Grandma gave Grandpa a push to send him on his way, but she held us back. "It's too heavy," she explained. "You'll get a hernia."

The airport vibrated with voices, and the floor was trampled by busy feet—sneakered, sandaled, and bare. Grandma paid close attention to all the different shoes, as if she were still in the shoe business on Flatbush Avenue in Brooklyn. People were waving and hugging and shouting orders to one another.

Soon Grandpa was back and the car was loaded. The night air felt nice and warm. On the sidewalk near Grandpa's car was a funny sight—a Florida Santa Claus wearing red Bermuda shorts and short sleeves was ringing a bell and ho-ho-hoing. His white hair and beard looked real and maybe the pot belly was, too.

Grandma got in the back seat with Marc, and I got

7

in the front and cuddled up close to Grandpa. So many good memories jumped into my head! Memories of birthday candles and my first ride on the BMT subway, and the day Grandpa showed me where Ebbets Field used to be. When Dad was a kid Grandpa would take him there to see a Dodgers baseball game and let him eat junk food. Memories from when Grandma and Grandpa lived only an hour's ride from Plainfield, New Jersey, where our house is. They'd visit us a lot. Grandma would take me shopping at a department store and complain about the drivers on Route 22. I realized how much I'd missed my grandparents. At least for this week everything would be the same as before, spending time with each other, listening to each other's news.

I turned around to look at Grandma. She was slim, the same as always, only with a tan. She wore a pants and blouse outfit and her nail polish and lipstick matched.

I turned back to the front, toward Grandpa. He has blue eyes like mine and a face that looks like it's smiling even when it's not. He'd put on a pound or two, and his stomach kind of got tucked under the steering wheel.

Grandpa reached over and patted my head. "You've grown, Stacy," he said. "You may not notice it but I can see."

"Thanks, Grandpa," I said, wishing I'd start to grow in a couple of important places as well. I rested my head against his shoulder.

Marc sneezed and Grandma leaned forward and poked Grandpa. "Turn off the air conditioner," she said. "He's getting a chill." Grandpa did just what Grandma said. In Brooklyn he used to do the opposite.

As we rode past a drive-in theater with eight screens, and lots of rent-a-car places, we answered questions—about Mom and Dad and Mom's new job as a real estate broker and what our parents gave us for Chanukah.

"I got a stereo and Marc got a digital watch. One big present for each of us because we'd be away and wouldn't get a present each day," I explained.

Grandpa smiled.

Just before we turned into the entranceway of Lemon Cove, I saw palm trees with Christmas lights. They looked so different from the Christmas trees I see in New Jersey.

"Here we are," Grandma said as we turned the corner.

A condominium was not what I had expected. Instead of rolling hills, it looked like a cement city. We drove past row after row of three-story buildings with numbered parking places in front and balconies in the back. That's about all I could see in the dark. We got into the elevator, which was wood paneled and smelled from lemon polish. The wood felt greasy when I touched it.

"Don't scrape the paneling with the suitcases," Grandma whispered. It was very quiet. It must have been very late, because Grandma worried that the elevator was making too much noise. We rode to the third floor and got out.

"This is called a catwalk," Grandpa whispered.

"Meow," Marc said as we walked down the long open walkway to the corner apartment.

"Sh," Grandpa said.

I ran my hand along the iron railing. My feet scraped against the cement, and Grandma's shoes tapped. Most of the windows we passed were dark. One had a picture of Santa Claus surfing painted on it. On each windowsill was an anttrap.

Grandma unlocked the door and pointed to a welcome mat. "With yellow carpet inside, it's important to wipe your feet."

Once inside the apartment we explored the three rooms. Everything looked new and cheerful, green and yellow and white. Everything matched. The bedspread matched the drapes in the bedroom. The dining area tablecloth matched the couch. Even the toilet paper in the bathroom was yellow and white flowered. I love when everything matches. In their Brooklyn house everything looked the same—old.

Grandma took off the lace tablecloth and put straw mats down. "You kids get ready for bed and I'll get some cookies out," she said.

After we'd changed into our pajamas we had milk and chocolate-chip cookies, but they were store-bought, not Grandma-made. "Be careful of crumbs. We don't want to get ants," Grandma said.

"We have so many new friends," Grandpa said, "and we got lots of advice about how to entertain our grandchildren. The Coopers' grandchildren are here already. What's his name, the one who used to be a dentist, his grandchildren are arriving tonight, too. But our friends Reggie and Joe—you'll meet them

tomorrow—their grandchildren aren't visiting this year."

"Everyone seemed to have suggestions for places to eat at and things to go see," Grandma added. She handed me another cookie and Grandpa poured more milk. They enjoyed watching us eat and listening as we talked—mostly complaints about school. She and Grandpa looked like they were chewing even though they were just watching—when I baby-sit for my cousin and feed the baby, I notice my own mouth moves, too.

"I'm glad you asked us to come," I said a few minutes later, helping Grandma tuck in the blankets on the two sofa beds.

"That's what this place is for," Grandpa said as he cleared the table. "A place for my kids to enjoy!"

Marc and I smiled at each other. We were sure ready to enjoy! We even had our bathing suits on under our pajamas. We each got under our covers. Grandma and Grandpa kissed us good night and turned out the lights. Then they went to their bedroom and closed the door.

I got up and got my postcards, pen, and flashlight. I always take a flashlight with me when I sleep away from home. It's a habit in case I'm bored and want to read newspapers and clip ads or articles or write letters after everyone's in bed. Marc was too tired, so I wrote the postcard home, then got back into the sofa bed. I wanted to have plenty of energy for the activities tomorrow.

As I dozed off I felt sure that we'd have a super vacation.

# 2
# DISAPPOINTMENTS

---

Dear Mom & Dad,

The airplane flight wasn't too bumpy. By the time you read this Marc & I will be filled with Grandma's oatmeal and swimming in the Florida sun. I can't wait. Thanks for letting us go.

Love,
Stacy (& Marc)

---

When I woke up on the morning of day two, I felt the way I do on the first day of summer vacation, like the whole world is sunny. I stretched and then snuggled back under the soft pink blanket. Grandma's blankets were brand-new. At home I sleep under a cotton comforter that the washing machine has chewed up.

I thought about how good it was not to race for a bus or need a late pass or worry if I was wearing the right thing or using the right words. My grandparents always think whatever I say or do is brilliant. As I listened for Grandma to be up I thought about how she used to cook us oatmeal in the morning on her old gas range in Brooklyn. The oatmeal never had lumps, and the steam would make my bangs curl. I was getting hungry. I figured she would probably cook some cereal as soon as she went into the kitchen, and then we'd go right to the pool.

I sat up and wiggled my toes in the yellow carpet. Boy, was it soft. At home in our ranch house our carpet's ten years old and we've vacuumed off the top layer. I sniffed. The apartment didn't smell like Grandma and Grandpa's old house in Brooklyn, with its steam heat and old books. Everything smelled new here, kind of like plastic and fresh paint. Whenever a closet was opened there was a strong smell of mothballs. "To keep out the dampness," Grandma had explained last night. The couches we'd slept on were in an L shape. Marc's was empty. I called him.

"I'm out here," he called back from the screened-in terrace. "There's a canal below . . . with ducks in it." Marc was ready to get going. He was wearing his quick-drying blue bathing suit. He is the kind of kid who likes to do things "immediately if not sooner," as my mother would say. The words he hates the most are "not now" and "later."

Grandma and Grandpa came out of their bedroom, but not in bathing suits. They were fully dressed and each had on white patent leather shoes— probably left over from their shoe store.

"Get dressed, kids," Grandpa said. "We'll take you to this great place for pancakes, and then we'll show you around the area."

Marc frowned. What we really wanted to do first thing was to dive into the pool. But we weren't about to spoil Grandpa's plans. I remembered plenty of times when they'd visit us in Plainfield, and I just had to show them my new earrings or my report on planets before they even took their coats off. I couldn't very well rush them now.

We dressed quickly. As we stepped outside and walked along the catwalk a warm breeze blew Marc's shoulder-length hair. Grandpa, who was walking behind us, said, "Still with the long hair? You and Stacy look alike from the back." He laughed. "I hope you both brought bathing caps." Marc and I laughed at his joke as we walked toward the elevator.

Grandpa and Grandma's friends, the Feldmans, lived two doors down the walkway. They were coming out of their doorway as we passed, so Grandpa invited them to come along. We had hoped we were going to have our grandparents to ourselves, but we weren't about to complain on our first day.

"Call us Joe and Reggie instead of Mr. and Mrs. Feldman or Aunt and Uncle," the woman said. "I hate when someone who is not related wants to be called Aunt This or That just because she's older," she added.

I liked Joe and Reggie right away.

In the car I sat in front between Grandma and Grandpa. Every now and then one or the other would kiss me. Marc and Joe and Reggie in the back were talking about mopeds, cameras, and tennis. I turned to look at them. Joe had gray hair that was almost white, and gentle, blue-gray eyes that told a people

15

watcher like me exactly how he was feeling. And his sparkling eyes told me he liked us. Reggie wore a leotard with a skirt over it. She said she was ready for her yoga class.

As we drove away, I took a good look at the condominium grounds. There were no trees we could pick oranges from for breakfast. No lemon trees, either, and the palm trees were tiny. The grass looked so neat—like even birds never walked on it. I got a glance at the pool as the car whizzed by. I could hardly wait to go swimming. It's my favorite thing to do.

But first we had this huge pancake breakfast. We sat in a big booth with cold seats. (Everything's air-conditioned in Florida: cars, restaurants, and apartments.) Grandpa called the restaurant the I-HOP. Oh, I'm not complaining. At home I never get to have whipped cream and strawberries on pancakes. But after breakfast, when I mentioned swimming, Grandma said we have to wait at least an hour until our food goes down.

"Why do we have to wait an hour?" I asked as we got back into the car.

"Cramps," Grandma answered. "We'll take a ride around town."

"On the swim team, we can't swim immediately after eating but we don't have to wait a full hour." I said.

"After whipped cream and strawberries it's an hour and that's that," Grandma said.

"We'll jog back," Joe said. "Reggie and I enjoy a

light breakfast and then some exercise. We'll see you later at the pool. I have to fix the stepladder there."

"Joe's Mr. Fix-it around Lemon Cove." Reggie laughed. "He loves to tinker around. He enjoys helping. I guess it's the fireman in him. That's what he used to be back in New York City, before he had to retire," she explained.

Joe and Grandpa paid the bill.

"Get some toothpicks," Grandma called. "We'll wait outside."

As Joe and Reggie jogged off, Reggie called, "Stop up and see us, kids; we're home any day but Monday, Wednesday, and Friday."

Grandpa tooted the horn as we rode past them. We rode and rode for about an hour, while Grandma and Grandpa pointed out about a hundred restaurants and described their salad bars. They showed us the medical center and the place where you can walk in and get your eyeglasses checked in five minutes. They also showed us a group of condominiums that looked like a ghost town because the builders had gone bankrupt and lots of old people had lost their life savings. And along the way they pointed out every shoe store.

"They don't know how to run a shoe business down here," Grandpa said.

"Our shoe store was much nicer," Grandma added. She held my hand and got a dreamy look. "Remember you used to visit us there and play with the foot measure?"

I said I did.

When a car honked behind us Grandpa rolled down the window and stuck his head out. "Go on— pass, you're in such a hurry. Me . . . I'm retired!"

Just when the hour was up, Grandma said we had to stop at the Winn Dixie to do food shopping. I was about to say "Now?" in my fresh voice, but Grandma added, "Just a few things to fill in, like milk, eggs, and bread. You kids sure drink a lot of milk. You'll have strong teeth."

In the supermarket I noticed Grandma opening the egg cartons. About half of them were missing some eggs.

She clicked her tongue. "End-of-the-month egg thieves they make out of old people, the government. Social Security money runs out and hungry people steal eggs."

I looked around, but I didn't see anyone stealing anything.

By the time we got back to the apartment it was a quarter to two.

"I can't wait to dive into the pool," Marc said. He is not the patient type. In fact he's the kind of kid who blows the horn on the car if Mom is in a store longer than one minute. He had been unbelievably good so far today. We were both ready to dive in. We still had our bathing suits on under our shorts.

"You can skip lunch," Grandma said. "You had such a big breakfast, and we eat dinner early here. Before six o'clock it's two dinners for the price of one at the restaurants, the early bird special."

I didn't understand what she meant. I thought we'd eat at the apartment. We never went out to eat a lot in Brooklyn—and it was the first night of Chanukah. We had to light the first candle.

"We'll meet you at the pool in a few minutes," Grandma added, handing us plastic-coated cardboard badges and pointing in the direction of the pool. "Pin these on your bathing suits." Then she said softly to Grandpa, "A few minutes early at the pool shouldn't matter." Grandpa shrugged his shoulders. I wondered what she meant and why we needed badges, but I didn't ask. The badges must be because we were strangers.

Then those words again: "Where are your bathing caps?" Grandma called. But we were on our way. "Shower first and don't splash," she added.

We rode down in the elevator, then walked across the grass toward the pool. It looked beautiful—clear water and plenty of room. It was empty. People were draped all around it, stretched out in assorted positions; some were trying to soak up every ray of sunlight, and others were trying to keep under the shade of a few umbrellas. A man with a towel over his head was positioning his back for the sun. A tall, thin, gray-haired man got up from a yellow and white chair and walked toward us. He had the kind of face like the ones carved in mountains out West someplace. (I once saw a picture of them in the *National Geographic*.) The man wore a block of wood on a string around his neck, and letters on the wood spelled out TED–POOL CAPTAIN. Before he spoke he sprayed his mouth with Binaca breath freshener. (I notice these things. My father says I'm very observant. My mother says she wishes I would observe how

19

to put a dish in the dishwasher instead of leaving it in the sink.) "Don't walk on the grass," the man called to us. Marc and I ran to get off the grass quickly.

"And don't run!" the man added.

"What are we supposed to do, fly?" I whispered to Marc.

"Let me see your passes," the pool captain demanded.

For a moment I felt like I was back in school, out in the hall during classes without a pass. In Plainfield Junior High that's a definite detention. But here at the pool I couldn't see how this guy Ted could miss seeing the passes, which were as big as an envelope. We pointed to our badges. We even stopped and let him read them. He looked like he thought they might be forged. Then we walked to the edge of the pool, and I stuck my toe in the water and was enjoying the cool, just-right feeling.

"We're supposed to shower," Marc said, turning toward the tiled shower. "Remember Grandma called out about it?"

"Wait a minute," the pool captain called in an unfriendly way. "Don't bother showering now." Then he added, "This is adult swim time from twelve noon to two thirty. You kids can't swim till after two thirty." He walked away. "It's a rule!" he called back over his shoulder. Ted's bony back was slumped forward, probably from the weight of the pool captain necklace.

Marc and I looked at each other in amazement. The pool was empty. "Wait till Grandma and Grandpa come down," I said. I figured they'd let us go in this empty pool. Grandma would do it nicely, but she'd stick up for us. She always did in Brooklyn, like a long time ago in the drugstore on Avenue J when the saleswoman yelled at me for trying out the sample lipsticks and powder.

Suddenly Ted called, "And you'd better have bathing caps to wear, both of you!" Grandpa hadn't been joking!

"I'm not wearing any bathing cap," Marc said to me, and he meant it. When Marc makes up his mind, there's no changing it. Even when he was little he was like that. In nursery school he said he wouldn't play circle games, and he never did. He only played games where you stood in a square.

Just then Grandma and Grandpa arrived. I couldn't believe it. They had to wear badges, too. Then I looked around and realized everyone was wearing a badge. And all the chairs were marked LEMON COVE RESIDENTS ONLY! and were chained to one another. You could stub your toe on the chains and hurt yourself.

Grandma put down a plastic bag filled with suntan lotion, sunglasses, needlepoint, and bathing caps. At least three different colored bathing caps showed through the clear plastic. Grandma spread a towel out on the lounge but didn't lie down, and Grandpa headed for a table at the other end. He started talking to the people sitting around it.

"Come, kids," Grandma said, pulling my hand. "I'll introduce you; then you can go for a swim. I'll probably have to drag you out of the pool, you'll love it so much." Grandma laughed and rumpled my hair.

Ted heard her last remark. "You'll have to drag them out because they're not allowed in yet!" he snapped. "You know that!" He turned like a soldier and marched away.

"Why can't we go in, anyway?" Marc asked. His patience was not going to hold out much longer.

"Maybe they put chlorine in it or something," Grandma said. "The pool is kept nice and clean here." Then she added proudly, "You don't even find hairs in it."

"You don't even find people in it," I said, waiting for her to stand up for us.

"Why do they keep kids out?" Marc asked, frowning.

"It's a new rule, special for over Christmas vacation," Grandma admitted. "Because other times there are only adults here." Grandma grabbed our hands and tugged. We were on our way. "Anyway, I want you to meet all our new friends," she said, changing the subject.

We walked over to the table with the open umbrella on it, where Grandpa was sitting, talking and pointing to us. A tiny but very strong woman gave us a friendly pinch. She smelled like a bottle of suntan lotion, and I think her name was Mrs. Libretti. At least twenty people hugged and measured us. Some of the men had bellies sticking out; some had hairy chests and bushy eyebrows. Some of the people looked like they exercised every day. Mrs. Roth had very crooked toes. (Sometimes my eye just catches on a detail like that because I'm a people watcher.) Grandma and Grandpa beamed as we smiled politely.

But now something had begun to bother me. What other people thought of us seemed more important than our not being able to swim. Grandma even introduced me as "My granddaughter, Stacy, who gets straight A's in school." Before, in Brooklyn, I'd been just Stacy. And my straight A's were last year, in grade school. In junior high I'd just slaved for every B. And then we all had to listen as this woman read out loud a letter from her granddaughter, a private letter. Suddenly I felt like I was in the middle of that science-fiction movie *Invasion of the Body Snatchers*, as if a strange being were living in my grandmother's body. I moved over to Grandpa.

"The pool captain said we can't go in until two thirty," I said. I just knew *he'*d take care of it, because he never could stand senseless rules back in Brooklyn. Sometimes he let us ring up the sales on the cash register in his store, even though we were underage.

"That's ridiculous," said Grandpa. "It's the hottest part of the day. Later it gets chilly." In December, even in Florida, it gets cool when the sun goes down. He shook his head. But he said all this to me, not to Ted.

"But it's the rule," said Grandma, looking around as if someone was watching her. A group of older kids walked by with a radio blaring rock music. Mrs. Roth with her crooked toes hobbled after them a few steps shouting, "Turn that music down!" But the kids had already disappeared around the corner. So she glared at two other kids minding their own business at the edge of the pool opposite us. "You kids don't respect anyone anymore!" she shouted at them.

Marc pointed to the boy and girl, who were dangling their feet in the water.

"Okay," Grandma said, as if giving in, "go dangle! It's only another half hour until two thirty, anyway. But don't sit on the pool steps." She pointed to the sign: SITTING ON POOL STEPS PROHIBITED.

A ripple of disappointment went through me. I had the feeling that if this pool was in Brooklyn, like at Brighton Private where Grandma used to take us, she would have said, "So, go in. It's empty anyway. What do we care what they think?" Yes, Grandma seemed different than she used to be. She didn't speak up, and it bothered me. Grandpa seemed different, too. He looked angrily at Ted, but only when Ted couldn't see. What good did that do? When would they stick up for us? And Grandpa kept spraying his mouth with Binaca breath spray. I'd never seen him do that before.

Marc and I sat down next to this blond boy and girl. They looked about our age; maybe the girl was a little younger than Marc. Anyway, they both seemed miserable. They weren't talking or laughing, or even kicking their feet. They just "dangled" and stared up at the clock.

"Hi," I said. "I'm Stacy Zimmerman and this is my brother, Marc. We just got here last night."

Marc slumped his shoulders and drummed his fingers on the edge of the pool.

"I'm Paul Cooper," the blond boy said with a smile. The sun sparkled on his braces. "And this is my sister, Lisa. We've been here three days already, and we've got eight days to go."

It sounded as if they were doing a prison sentence.

24

"You don't seem to be having a very good time," I said. "We couldn't wait to get down here. We've got so many plans. We're going to have a ball."

"You can have a ball, as long as you don't bounce it or throw it," Paul said, pretending to read something. He smiled, then frowned. "This is torture for me," he added. "I'm on the swim team at my community pool. In Morristown, New Jersey."

"Hey," I said, "I swim for our Community Center team in Plainfield. We're practically neighbors!"

Some more kids sat down on the opposite side of the pool. Three girls who had white bathing caps and red and white striped bathing suits looked like tubes of toothpaste, the way they were sitting. And a boy near them twirled a bathing cap on his finger. Everyone looked bored. At a nearby table another group of kids were playing cards. A card suddenly blew into the pool and Ted quickly got a net on a long stick and scooped the card out as if it was the biggest, grossest spider or something. As he tossed it at the kids he said, "Keep your garbage out of the pool."

Marc leaned over the water and started to splash himself. "I'm steaming," he said. "By now even that shower looks good."

"Yeah," said Lisa, "and I hate showers. I only take baths at home." She twisted her long blond hair into a knot and held it with her left hand. "And don't anybody splash me. I hate it." She glared at Marc.

"Why don't we go into the showers until it's two thirty?" I suggested. By then I'd have done anything to cool off, too. I got up, brushing at a spot where I'd scraped my thigh on the cement.

We all walked over to the two showers. Paul and I were going to use them first. On the way over I noticed that Paul was taller than I am, but not by much. And he had blond, fuzzy hairs on his back. The kids sitting on the other side of the pool just watched us.

In the shower I pretended I'd been on a desert for a month, and I let the cold water drip down my face. (I've got a good imagination. I'm much spunkier on the inside than on the outside.) The water made me feel better. Maybe Grandma and Grandpa only seemed different because I hadn't seen them for so long.

When Paul and I got out of the showers Lisa and Marc went in. Marc pretended it was a torture chamber with stinging needles. "I'll talk," he said, and he made up a name, rank, and serial number. Lisa giggled. Suddenly we heard a yell.

"Stop fooling around with those showers!"

I looked around. It wasn't even that pool captain, Ted, who had shouted. It was some really thin lady with white ointment on her nose and lips and a bright pink and purple flowered scarf on her head. "You're wasting water," she added, her hands on her hips.

"I don't believe this," Marc said as he brushed the water from his eyes.

We all walked toward the pool. Grandma and Grandpa waved to us and pointed to the clock. It was two thirty.

Without even thinking about it I dove in like I always do on the swim team. When I came to the top, about twelve people were standing around the pool glaring at me. I looked down to see if maybe my bathing suit had fallen off. Marc came up next to me, and everyone started scowling at him, too. Grandma ran over to us waving two bathing caps. One had pink rubber flowers on it. Behind her Ted pointed a long, crooked finger at a sign that said NO DIVING.

Lisa was still putting on her bathing cap. She had a lot of long hair to stuff in. Paul's hair was regular neck length, and no one seemed to be bothering him. He was swimming laps—he had a good stroke, too.

I swam to the edge and put my hand out to grab a dangling bathing cap from Grandma. Ted, the pool captain, pointed at Marc.

"He needs one, too. Shoulder-length hair, the rule says."

Neither Grandma nor Grandpa said a word to help Marc, even though his eyes pleaded with them and he had been so extra patient.

"I'm not wearing any bathing cap," Marc bellowed. And he swam away.

I looked around at the people at the pool. They seemed to be signaling with their eyes, like silent Morse code. The message was clear: TROUBLE AHEAD.

# 3
# ENOUGH IS
# ALMOST ENOUGH

---

Dear Mom and Dad,

The pool looks nice. The restaurants have good food. We met two nice kids named Lisa and Paul. The tennis courts look nice. Grandma and Grandpa look nice. Everything looks nice.

Love,
Stacy (& Marc)

P.S. Grandma and Grandpa liked the subscription to Holiday Magazine we gave them for Chanukah. They thought it was nice.

---

The morning of day three we were still hopeful, because the night before had been pretty good. We'd lit the shammes candle and used it to light one Chanukah candle. Then we watched them melt. Grandma and Grandpa took us on a moonlight cruise for our present. We thought our plane tickets were an expensive gift so we weren't expecting any presents, but Grandpa said our being in Florida was like giving a gift to themselves.

The cruise was beautiful, and there were a restaurant and a dance band right on the boat. Grandma and Grandpa have learned all the latest dances and they were enjoying showing us. It was a "pacemaker disco," Grandpa said. They discussed all the shoes people were wearing as if they were still in that business. And we got to talk a little about New Jersey and our swim team when the band took a break. But when Marc went to the men's room Grandma said, "Stacy, you tell Marc to wear the bathing cap in the pool. He'll listen better if it comes from you, okay?" Without waiting for an answer, she and Grandpa got up to dance.

This morning Grandpa insisted on taking us to this place where a lot of people from Lemon Cove eat breakfast.

"They even serve strawberry cream cheese to smear on bagels," he said.

Before we could say we'd rather eat in, he told us he'd arranged to meet some friends there and we were a little late already. At the restaurant Grandpa led us to the table where his friends were. Everyone talked about diets and "early bird specials" and one hundred ways to make eggs. Marc and I looked at each other across the table and at the same time mouthed the word BORING. We wished Joe was here to talk to. But Grandpa had said Reggie and Joe weren't around today, though he didn't say where they went.

We were polite, even though I'd rather have talked

to Grandma about my latest report card, or about the Plainfield Junior High School dance I wasn't asked to, or about anything. I wished I'd brought a newspaper to clip from.

"Eat," Grandma said to me. "And Marc, use a knife, not your finger." I didn't mind too much, but I could tell Marc was about to be fresh—he started cracking his knuckles.

"I think Grandma's just following what she's seen other grandparents do," I whispered to him. "Like you did whatever I did the first time we went to camp."

"They're acting dumb, Stacy," Marc said, spreading more cream cheese with his finger.

Actually, I figured Grandma wanted to impress her friends. But she never used to be like that. Marc was right. It did seem dumb. Still, I was glad the siren of a passing ambulance had drowned out his words.

On our way out of the restaurant I saw Ted at a table in the corner, dumping a basket of leftover rolls into a plastic bag. Then he ordered the waitress to give him a basket with rolls in it. I don't think he saw me.

Outside the air-conditioned restaurant the Florida sun felt like a hot slap in the face. The car was like an oven till the air conditioner was on. Grandpa just had to drive a mile or so out of the way to show us this model all-electric house. Frankly, I didn't see what was so great about it. With all the blackouts we'd been having every summer, this house of the future would soon have all the conveniences of a log cabin. I wished Grandma and Grandpa would just take us to the pool and settle the cap issue themselves. I was not going to be the one to make Marc put on a bathing cap. There are moments when he is a pain, like when I had a slumber party and he put plastic bugs in our sleeping bags, but he never did anything to deserve this cap stuff.

Grandpa dropped Grandma off at the beauty parlor, which had a sign in the window: NO HUSBANDS ALLOWED. "Some of the men follow their wives everywhere," Grandpa explained. "They have nothing to do. Me, I play cards."

But instead of driving to the condominium, Grandpa gave us money and dropped us off at the afternoon movie show. "You'll enjoy it," he said. "A lot of other grandparents drop their kids at the movie theater. Some friends at the pool told me how much fun you'll have at the movies." I hoped it was the Coopers and that maybe we'd at least meet Paul and Lisa—especially Paul. But if they were there I didn't see them.

Back in Brooklyn Grandpa would have stayed with us at the Kingsway movie theater on Kings Highway. He would have munched popcorn and bought us junk food to "fill up on." Then Grandma would yell at him when we'd get back and he'd smile. Instead, today he was going to the rec room at the clubhouse to play cards. I was beginning to wonder why Grandpa hadn't taken us inside the rec room. He had only shown us the outside of the clubhouse.

The movie turned out to be pretty good, so we didn't mind. Only we could have seen lots of science fiction movies in the South Plainfield Shopping Mall, and we had special plans for Florida but one by one they were being ruined. After the movies, since we'd skipped lunch, we went for an "early bird" dinner, again at the place with shrimp in their salad bar and shells and nets on the walls. Of course we met more of Grandma and Grandpa's friends, but not Paul and Lisa Cooper or their grandparents.

"This is Mr. Rudolph and his lady friend, Mrs. Stein," Grandma whispered, explaining that Mrs. Stein's husband had died last year. "Mr. Rudolph and Mrs. Stein live together," Grandma continued. "They're waiting for their children's approval to get married. It's a problem with wills and Social Security. They have a Ping-Pong table at their house and we're going there so you can use it," Grandma added, talking louder. I'd rather have used the Ping-Pong table in the rec room but no one asked my opinion about anything anymore. Mr. Rudolph and Mrs. Stein held hands, and he called her princess.

"What about the Chanukah candles?" Marc asked, kind of pulling at Grandma's sleeve like he used to when he was little.

"We'll skip tonight," Grandma said. "I'll just tell you what your gift is—rubber slippers for by the pool so you won't get a fungus." Marc shifted his weight from foot to foot with a sigh.

In Brooklyn Grandma and Grandpa would never have skipped lighting Chanukah candles, not even one night. I don't like things to change, especially not grandparents and holidays. I still even keep my stuffed animals lined up on my bed in the same order.

When we got to the Rudolph and Stein house I asked for a newspaper I could read and clip things from—my boredom remedy. Marc and I laughed at one ad I found. It said

UNWANTED HAIR

REMOVED

CERTIFIED ELECTROLOGISTS

733–2026

I poked Marc. "That's another answer to the bathing cap problem. Maybe I ought to give this ad to Ted." I stuffed it in my pocket. Marc poked me back.

Grandpa raised his eyebrows. "Behave, you two. Go play Ping-Pong." But these ads were too funny to leave. I clipped another one that said

REPEL FLEAS NUTRITIONALLY

LEARN ABOUT HEARTWORMS,

TICKS, INSECTICIDAL EFFECTS.

SATISFACTION GUARANTEED.

Then it gave an address.

"Repel fleas nutritionally?" I joked to Marc. "Does that mean eat them?" We both started to giggle. Grandpa handed us the Ping-Pong paddles and pointed to the table.

"Leave them be," Mrs. Stein said. "They're having fun. It's good to hear children's laughter. It's usually quiet enough around here."

"The princess is right," Mr. Rudolph agreed and

went on showing Grandma all the Chatahootchie tile he put down on the floor of the Florida room, which looked like a screened-in porch with a pebble floor.

I figured the next day had to be better.

But the morning of day four, when I asked, "Can we play tennis this morning?" Grandpa changed the subject.

"There's this terrific omelet place," he said. "You've got to try it."

The only reason Marc didn't make a fuss was that I paid him a dollar. My grandpa's worth it, I figured. But Marc was not happy to see green things wrapped up in a swollen scrambled egg. I like strange foods—I even eat artichokes—so an avocado-tomato omelet tasted good to me. This restaurant had butcher block tables and a newspaper machine at the door. The headline read: SNOW HITS THE NORTH. As we left, Grandpa put a quarter in the machine, opened the glass window, and took out a newspaper, which he handed to me. Maybe he figured Marc and I would spend the day clipping ads and not want to go to the pool.

Grandpa put the radio on in the car. Just as I was about to talk, he said, "Sh, it's the weather report. They're telling about all that snow up North and how it's eighty degrees and sunny here in Fort Lauderdale." I didn't listen. I found a funny ad in the paper and showed it to Marc. It said

FULL SERVICE DENTAL OFFICE
BUDGET DENTURES

"I guess in Florida a lot of people can just drop off their teeth." Marc got a pain in his stomach from holding back his laughter.

Back at Lemon Cove, Marc and I put on our bathing suits, but Grandma and Grandpa stayed dressed. "We'll skip the pool today," Grandpa said. "We're going to take a little nap. But you two go ahead and enjoy."

"And wear your new rubber shoes and these." Grandma handed me two bathing caps, a blue one with a design in the rubber and a pink flowered one.

Grandma and Grandpa were not going to go with us and stick up for us. I still didn't say anything, but more and more I was thinking that these were not the same grandparents I used to know in Brooklyn. Why did they have to be different? It really bothered me. I wondered if you know when you're changing. Did they know? Would I know? I looked down at my body. The only changes I wanted wouldn't come.

Marc ran ahead to the elevator, his rubber thongs flapping. I raced down the steps and beat him. At the pool one group of grown-ups was talking loudly to an adult guest, a man about forty, like my father. The man's face and arms were lobster red with sunburn, and he wasn't wearing a hat. He was getting annoyed, turning redder. Each person was giving different directions to Route I–95. Another group was arguing about something called a rec lease, whatever that is.

They kept shouting and interrupting each other. We met Paul and Lisa and we sat down near some other kids to dangle until two thirty. We were going to obey *that* rule.

At two twenty-five kids came out of the buildings like worms after a rain. There must have been about twenty. The ones that were about to go in the pool wore bathing caps.

At two thirty, when we stepped out of the showers, everyone was watching us to see what we would do today. I put on the pink flowered bathing cap, though I let some hair stick out on purpose. But Ted was already motioning to Marc and shouting, "Bathing cap!" I don't know what Marc would have done if Joe hadn't arrived on his moped.

Joe's gray hair was blowing in the breeze and his shirt was open and flapping. His moped whirred softly. Instead of going into the pool, Marc walked over to Joe. Paul, Lisa, and I followed, leaving Ted, the pool captain, and about six other people arguing about us.

Joe turned the motor off. "Finally getting to fix the ladder today," he said to us as he walked to the pool. "I've been real busy with something else," he added. In a few minutes he came back. "I'll have to go to the hardware store and get some screws to fix this. I'll clean the filter next week," he said to some people sitting nearby.

"Want to climb up on the seat of my moped?" he asked me. He didn't mind that I was still wet from the shower. "Good to see you kids," he said.

"Good to see you, too," I said, and the other kids

agreed. I climbed onto the moped. Joe had a walkie-talkie radio hanging from the handlebar and Marc was most interested in that.

A woman's lively voice came over the radio. "Got your ears on, Gray Rider?"

"Ten-four, Painter Lady," answered Joe, speaking into the microphone. "That's my wife Reggie's C.B. handle. She likes to oil paint, so that's why she took the name Painter Lady."

"I like to draw and paint, too," I mumbled. Usually I don't tell people that. It just kind of popped out with Joe.

"Reggie will be glad to hear that," he said.

"What's your ten-twenty?" said Painter Lady.

"Poolside," Joe said into the C.B.

Then he turned to us. "Reggie worries about me when I ride this moped by myself," Joe explained. "The C.B. lets her know I'm safe. When you're old like us, you depend on each other a lot."

Joe glanced around. "What's going on here, anyway?" he said, pointing to the group of people of assorted shapes who kept looking over at Marc.

When Marc started to explain, an odd thing happened. Joe listened to us. He was different from the other people we'd met. He didn't just talk, he really listened. "I'm not going to wear a bathing cap, even if I never swim again," said Marc, and his ears got red with anger. "I don't have to wear a cap at the pool in New Jersey, and it's just as clean there."

"We took a shower. We waited for the right time," I added. "We tried to obey, but there are even more rules here than in school."

Then Paul added, "You haven't seen anything yet. Wait till you see the rec room rules."

"You can't see the rec room rules *or* the rec room," said Lisa, and she shifted her weight from one foot to another. "You're not allowed in it if you're under eighteen. My grandma said. She should know. Grandma and Grandpa are always in the rec room playing bridge. Before they moved here they used to play Go Fish with us. Remember, Paul?" Lisa twisted her bathing suit strap as she talked.

"I love to play Go Fish," Joe said, and Lisa smiled.

"You mean we can't play Ping-Pong or use the pool table or art room?" I asked Joe. One by one our plans were being blown to bits.

"I'm afraid the kids are right," said Joe. "You can't use the rec room, but you could use Painter Lady's art room if you like. Any day except Monday, Wednesday, or Friday. We'd love your company and we're just two doors down from your grandparents, Stacy."

"That's really nice," I said, and even though Joe was practically a stranger, I reached out and touched his arm, just because I felt like it. I wondered where he and Reggie went on Monday, Wednesday, and Friday, but I was too shy to ask.

Just then I noticed Ted, the pool captain, staring at us.

"I'm beginning to feel like a criminal at age thirteen," I said. I felt like pedaling real fast on the moped but I didn't want to break it.

Joe looked at me. His eyes stopped sparkling and grew as sad as a cocker spaniel puppy's. He put his hand gently on my shoulder. "That's just how my grandchildren felt last Christmas. This year they didn't want to come here at all."

"Who makes up all the rules?" I asked. I snapped the rubber band on my braces. Sometimes I do that when I'm angry.

"I don't think anyone knows anymore," Joe muttered.

"Why is that Ted so mean to us kids?" Paul asked.

"He could tell us the rules in a nice way," Lisa added in a low voice. "Does he have arthritis? When my grandma talks mean she says, 'Sorry, it's my arthritis.'"

I got off the moped and wiped off the seat with my hand.

"He's not a bad guy," Joe explained as he got on the motor bike. "Ted was a waiter all his life. I guess now he wants to give orders instead of taking them."

I laughed because that sounded like something I would come up with. And it told me Joe was a people watcher, too. Thoughts were clicking in my head like a computer terminal. NO DIVING, NO USING THE REC ROOM, CRAZY POOL HOURS, NO WALKING ON THE GRASS, NO SITTING ON THE FOR-RESIDENTS-ONLY CHAIRS, NO THIS, NO THAT! NO SENSE!—the grandma and grandpa from Brooklyn should have realized that.

"Gray Rider, do you read me?" the voice boomed from the speaker on Joe's C.B.

"Starting my flip-flop now." Joe added, "Put the coffee on. And kids, don't forget to visit us." That was important to Joe—his eyes were sparkling again.

41

He waved as he took off, leaving a slight smell of exhaust and three ladies standing by the pool saying, "Shush, what a racket," and "P.U. What a smell!" I thought perhaps Joe revved the engine one last time on purpose.

I turned to Lisa, admiring the way her face told her feelings. Lips squeezed to one side meant she was annoyed, and she opened her eyes wide when she was excited. Well, at least we'd made some nice friends.

"Do you guys play tennis?" I asked, remembering another of our special plans. Maybe the day could be saved yet.

"We'd like to," Paul said, "but you have to sign up for a court." His usually straight shoulders sagged.

"So let's go sign up," Marc said, happy to avoid the bathing cap issue for a while.

"Easier said than done," said Lisa. "You have to sign up in the rec room." She pointed at a modern white building up the road and made a droopy face that said "Don't bother."

"So let's sign up," I said.

"Not possible," said Paul. "Remember the rules? If you're under eighteen you're not allowed in the rec room."

This was getting to be a bit too much. "There's strength in numbers," I muttered.

As we started off, moving fast but not really running, one man in red flowered bathing trunks said, "Wild animals, these kids, running back and forth and back and forth."

A woman with a floppy hat and a nice smile answered, "You were never a child?" I wished my grandma and grandpa had heard that.

Another man with a cigar in the corner of his mouth turned to his neighbor and said, "Ants in their pants, they've got?" Ted shouted, "DON'T RUN!"

We started to walk slowly, but—we walked *on the grass*. It did our hearts good (and it didn't really hurt anything). I hopped over the NO WALKING ON THE GRASS sign. This was our first rebellious act! But it was only a token protest. I was still determined to hang on and make the most of things, so instead of invading the rec room right then and there, we decided to calm down and cool off a bit. We headed up to Grandma and Grandpa's apartment. We were going to speak up about our feelings, but when we got there we changed our minds.

"How nice," Grandma said at the door. "You brought friends to visit. You're the Coopers' grandchildren, aren't you? You're all enjoying, I'm sure. Come in. I'll make you all a treat. Just wipe your feet, kids—yellow carpet," she said, as if that explained everything.

Wiping our bare feet on the mat seemed kind of funny. We giggled. It also reminded me that we'd left our rubber thongs at the pool.

"Go sit down on the terrace with Grandpa," Grandma called.

Grandpa was sitting on a lounge chair reading the *Broward Jewish Journal*. "I'm relaxing," he said.

"Egg creams," Grandma announced, pushing a tray of brown, foamy drinks through the pass-thru window to the terrace.

43

How could I complain about a few rules when now it felt like old times in Brooklyn?

"I found a place that has Fox's U-Bet Chocolate Syrup, just like at home, and real spritz bottles of seltzer like in Brooklyn," Grandma explained as she joined us. When she said "home" and "Brooklyn" she got a sound like a shiver in her voice.

"Eggs in chocolate syrup?" Lisa made a face that meant "You're grossing me out."

Paul tasted his drink right away.

"It's a Brooklyn drink," I said. "It's called an A cream, but everyone says it egg cream. There's no eggs in it, just chocolate syrup, a drop of milk, and seltzer—club soda. It's delicious."

"We used to get them from Sam's, the corner candy store, next to my grandma and grandpa's shoe store," Marc added. He drank his. I drank mine. Lisa watched, then finally drank hers.

"It's super," she admitted.

Grandpa got up and went into the living room. When he came back out he handed us a deck of cards. But he wasn't going to play with us. He went back to reading the paper . . . and relaxing.

The drinks had calmed us down a little, but not completely. We didn't play gin rummy. We played war!

# 4
# ENOUGH IS
# DEFINITELY ENOUGH

The evening of day four turned out a lot better. While reading the *Broward Jewish Journal*, Grandpa had found an ad for a restaurant with, of course, an exceptionally good "early bird special" that included as many potato pancakes as you could eat. For some reason this reminded him of his friend Herb, who I guess loves potato pancakes.

Grandpa said he felt so relaxed he could even enjoy an evening with Herb, and why not take him out to dinner instead of eating at home? Grandma thought it was a wonderful idea.

"Herb lives alone in his own apartment," she said, clicking her tongue.

"What are you clicking about? He's happy enough. Women chase after him like he was a Hollywood big shot," Grandpa said. "He's a Gray Panther. He marches in protests and writes lots of letters to improve things for old people." I thought he sounded interesting.

"He's a gray, long-haired hippie," Grandpa joked. "Marc will love him."

Grandma said having potato pancakes out would

45

be a good way to celebrate the third night of Chanukah. I certainly didn't agree, and to make matters worse, our presents for that night were white bathing caps that made you look like the Conehead family on TV.

I asked if I could light the shammes and the three candles and Grandma said yes, but I'd have to blow them out before we left. In Brooklyn we wouldn't have left. We would have watched the colored candles disappear. I remembered the time I lit the Chanukah candles when I was three and made a wish like I'd been told to do on birthdays. When I wished for a Christmas tree, Grandma had shown me all the beautiful colors of the Chanukah candles and hugged and kissed me. Now I felt like I wanted to show them to her.

We picked Herb up and drove for a very long time to the restaurant. Grandpa said the potato pancakes were the best he's had in ages. I didn't see why he didn't just ask Grandma to make some, since hers are better.

For a people watcher like me, Herb was a prize. He'd pound on the table when he talked about nursing homes and abuse of the elderly. Every dish on the table shook. Grandma had to grab the saltshaker before it fell. Herb really did have almost shoulder-length hair like Marc's, only it was gray. He kept pushing it off his forehead. The very top of his head was sort of bald, though.

"If we're not going to help ourselves, who's going to help us older people? We got plenty of votes, you

46

know!" Herb was talking and talking. He only stopped now and then to eat a bite of potato pancake. He put sour cream on his. (I'm an applesauce lover myself.)

"We're an action group, us Gray Panthers. We don't want anyone telling us we have to retire," Herb said, "and we need better transportation. We'll stand on the tracks or stop buses with wheelchairs, even! If we have to."

"Calm down, Herb," Grandma said. "You won't digest. Potato pancakes can lie like a lump on your chest and you'll be up all night."

"So I'll get up and write letters to the governor or congress," he said, taking a bite of a veal chop. "I'll listen to a Mozart record for inspiration. Just because I was an accountant working with numbers doesn't mean I can't learn to work with words. And I'll use numbers too—statistics and stuff."

"So they'll file the letter—right in the garbage pail," Grandpa added.

"Not when they know it's from the Gray Panthers," Herb said.

I looked back and forth from Herb to Grandpa like at a tennis match. Even Marc was listening.

"We've got young and old working together and that equals power," Herb said, pounding the table again. This time Grandma had to mop up a spill from her water glass. "We're gonna change society," he said. "Look around down here. They want to keep the elderly out of the way playing bingo and shuffleboard. That's what Maggie Kuhn says: 'We're being treated unfairly . . . like kids.'"

"Who's Maggie Kuhn?" I asked. Herb sounded al-

47

most mean. I get that way, too, when I think some-one's been unfair to me.

"Maggie's the founder of the Gray Panthers, and she's no youngster herself," Herb added.

When the waitress tried to clear the table before Herb was finished he practically stabbed her hand with his fork.

"We can question the government and big business and whoever we damn please! We've got time on our side because so what if we take risks? What have we got to lose?" he added—pounding again.

"Right on," Marc said. Herb roughed up Marc's long hair and smiled for the first time.

That night was really interesting. We had all the potato pancakes we could eat—I ate four and Marc ate five. They were good, but Grandma's are better. I liked Herb. He was so full of energy. I forgot he was old. He said Marc and I could join the Gray Panthers, too, and whispered to me, "Your grandparents should come to one of our meetings." He seemed to be telling me to work on them.

After dinner Herb took all of us on a ride on one of the new buses that lower so old people can step on and off easily. He said letters and Gray Panther dem-onstrations had got it. After we drove Herb home, instead of good-bye, he said, "If you put all the colors of the rainbow together, you get gray—everyone gets old." And he kind of saluted and walked up the path. He walked tall even though he limped.

The morning of day five was too boring to even tell much about—but the afternoon made us want to scream! It was exciting and terrible at the same time.

The day started out with breakfast at the bank, believe it or not.

"Let's go to the bank that has donuts and coffee," Grandma suggested. We were all on the terrace. It was another warm day. "We have to take care of the C.D.'s today, before the interest rates drop."

"Certificate of Deposit," Grandpa explained, showing me an ad in the newspaper. "Whatever I earn in interest rates I put in a bank for your college," he said, and he looked at Marc and me with pride.

I kissed his forehead.

Grandma and Grandpa seemed to enjoy getting all their papers and bankbooks together and talking about Jessica, their banker, as if she were a close friend. They looked like they used to at the shoe store when they closed out the register and checked receipts at the end of the day. "This is important business," Grandma said.

"Because of inflation," Grandpa added.

By 9:00 we were at the bank. It had gardens and benches inside, and on one side of the big room there was a long table with a big coffee maker—like at back-to-school night when the parents visit and have cookies and coffee and stuff in the school lunchroom. At the end of this table was a big box for people to donate old eyeglasses.

A lot of old people were standing around the table greeting each other as if they came here every morning for breakfast. This guy with powdered sugar on his mustache and donut jelly in the corner of his mouth said to a little guy wearing a lime green outfit, "You oughta go down to Atlantic Federal. They got bagels and lox.''

Breakfast at the bank was pretty bad, but the afternoon at the condominium was worse: big trouble.

I guess someone had readjusted the lawn sprinkler heads so that when they went on, the entire row of people sitting by the pool got soaked.

"My hairdo's ruined," cried Mrs. Roth with the crooked toes (now nail-polished).

"What do these kids want from our lives!" a man cried out from behind a very soggy *Miami Herald*.

Paul and Lisa were just coming out of the elevator, so Marc and I waited for them at the poolside. We'd just gotten there ourselves. That bank business had seemed to take forever. We'd even had to go to another bank that was giving out drinking glasses and ice buckets decorated like gas station pumps. I couldn't figure out the connection, but if you opened an account—even just a dollar—you got this free gift. "You'll take it back for your mother and father," Grandma had said.

We'd only been down at the pool for a couple of minutes when the sprinkler incident happened. We couldn't help laughing. It was a funny sight. But it was Marc and Paul and Lisa and me who ran over to turn the sprinklers off.

So we were surprised now when Ted yelled at us. "Out!" he shouted. "You are not to come back to this pool without your grandparents *and* without bathing caps on your heads." Maybe because of my people-watching habit, I was the only one who saw an older woman in the corner laughing. Something told me she had turned on the sprinklers, but I couldn't prove it. Maybe we looked suspicious, but this is America: Whatever happened to innocent until proven guilty? I was beginning to feel what my dad calls "rebellious."

Marc came really close to turning the sprinkler on right in Ted's face. But he didn't. "Come on, you guys," he said to us, and we stalked away to join another group of kids at a table with an umbrella. We just sat there and complained about how everything here was unfair.

The other girl—I didn't know her name—pounded her fist like Herb. She told how she was chased off the shuffleboard court because she'd make it dirty with her sneakers. And the other guy said he'd won pool tournaments and everything out on Long Island, but here he couldn't even go in the rec room. Even his own grandparents told him he might tear up the pool table, and they know he's got his own pool table in his basement at home. They gave it to him!

And where were our grandmother and grandfather during all this? They were still upstairs "getting their papers in order."

That's when Marc and Paul and Lisa and I decided to check out the rec room and try to reserve a tennis court for tomorrow. Our vacation was half over already, and we hadn't even been swimming more than once, or played tennis or anything. Our plans were really going down the drain. One thing after another. All these rules and orders from people were really getting unbearable.

We walked over to the rec room. (On the grass of

51

course—what did it matter? The people thought we'd been on the grass playing around with the sprinkler anyway.) The other kids didn't follow us. They were under orders like pet poodles to sit and stay.

Paul and Lisa had told us all about the rec room rules and not being allowed in. They hadn't exaggerated—not one bit. When we got there, a man chased us out of the entranceway, an area lined with bulletin boards filled with notices and rules. The man sat behind a small wooden desk. He pointed his crooked finger to a sign that said UNDER 18 NOT ALLOWED. Waving us out with a flick of his wrist, he added, "Rules are to be followed."

That was exactly the problem around here. Whether the rules made sense or not, everyone followed them, including my very own grandparents. I tried hard to figure out why. (My mother says the first letter I learned as a baby was *Y* and I've been saying it ever since.) I remember that when I first got into junior high I wanted so much to fit in that I even laughed at a girl who wore her pants too short, just because the other kids laughed. I didn't feel too good about that afterward. I figured that sometimes people stop thinking in a new place, and just follow. That thought gave me a rebellious idea, which I filed away in my mind.

"Excuse me," I said, being extra polite just for spite. "We're trying to follow the rules. We want to sign up for the tennis court."

"The owners of the apartment must sign you up themselves in person between six and seven in the evening," the man said and went back to reading his newspaper.

That was ridiculous. Tonight would be our first home cooked dinner. We'd be in the middle of watching the Chanukah candles and eating Grandma's chicken. I hoped. I'd hinted at it when Grandma mentioned dinner plans. I even gave her that recipe I'd clipped at the airport, the one for almond chicken. But I didn't really ask. In Brooklyn I would have said, "Cook chicken tonight, Grandma, please." I felt different here, too.

"Couldn't we just save our grandparents a trip down here?" Marc asked.

"We're going out for dinner," Paul said. "We always go out for dinner. Grandpa retired from being a printer and Grandma retired from cooking." He looked at me and muttered, "That's why we haven't played tennis yet. We're never here to sign up."

Lisa puffed her cheeks with an angry breath and gave what my mom would call a look that kills. She has these big eyes that send messages.

I figured I'd give it one last try to do things peacefully. "We've explained the problem. Couldn't you please let us sign up now?"

"N-o!" said the man. "And don't talk fresh to me." He waved a finger in my face. "You bend a rule and the next thing you know everyone wants you to bend it till it breaks." He was getting so excited that his last words came out in a spray. He got up, pushed the newspaper aside, and walked into the main room.

My heart was pounding. I was clenching my teeth together so tightly I thought I'd break my braces.

"Look at the bulletin board," Marc whispered. "More pages of rules. They must have to keep their dogs on a diet around here," he laughed. " 'NO DOG MAY WEIGH OVER 12 POUNDS.' "

Paul laughed, too, quietly. As he and Lisa read more rules, the man with the crooked finger came back.

"Now what are you troublemakers doing?" he said.

I couldn't resist. "I'm studying," I said, and I pretended to read some more.

He couldn't think of anything to say, I guess, so he walked inside the main room, to a lady who was knitting. I think she was the same lady with the white stuff on her nose at the pool the other day. She was sitting in a very pretty double-seater red chair on brass wheels. He pointed to us and said to her, "See? They're destroying already."

"To him touching something on a bulletin board is destroying," I whispered to Marc. That guy reminded me of a teacher in my school who thinks everyone cheats. All I once said to this kid was, "Do you have a pencil?" And this teacher repeated, counting each word on his fingers, "Do you have a pencil. That's five words. You must mean you want the answer to number five on the test. You can't fool me." I wish I'd had the nerve to talk back then. But I hadn't. Maybe that's why I was doubly mad now.

I peeked inside the main room, which was huge and beautiful. It smelled like an air-conditioned theater. A color TV and cozy black and white striped couches were in one corner. Nearby there were red velvet double-seater chairs on big brass wheels. There were rooms with doors marked CARDS, SEWING, ART, and LIBRARY. The main room had shiny waxed wood floors like a skating rink and there were red shag area rugs. Polished Ping-Pong tables and pool tables without a speck of dust—all without a single person using them.

It looked like such a terrific place. We were drooling like a baby that sees a cookie, but we couldn't use anything in the building. The man shooed us out of the rec room and closed the doors while we stood there. And I, the kid who has a poster in her room that says IT'S YOUR WORLD, IT'S MY WORLD, TAKE CARE OF IT, found myself wanting to litter, rip out flowers, or at least take one of the many pages of rules, rip it to shreds, and throw it in the air.

That grouchy man had told the lady with the knitting needles that we were "destroying." We were already in trouble about the sprinklers and we were innocent. If the people thought those things anyway, then it really didn't matter what we did.

"That man just taught me something," I said. "Rules that won't bend crack all by themselves. We've got to do something." I snapped the rubber bands on my braces. We got into a huddle. I thought of Herb and the Gray Panthers. Sometimes kids have to "help themselves" too! We all activated our brains. And the rebellion began! No one actually decided what we would do. It's just that we felt like volcanos about to erupt. We looked at each other and headed right for those big, wooden rec room doors, eight hands outstretched and pushing.

Once inside we really went wild. Marc was imitating a machine gun noise. He held his arm out stiffly in front of him and pointed a finger as he pulled on his thumb trigger.

Paul pushed me into a big red velvety rolling chair. It was the chair next to the lady with the knitting needles. Her eyeglasses fell right off her nose onto her lap as Paul started pushing my chair faster and faster, making a whirring sound on the waxed wood floor. After he steered around the shag rug, he hopped on beside me and we rode to the door marked ART. It didn't hurt the chairs or the floor one bit, and "action," as Herb had called it, sure helped us feel better. The knitting lady grabbed her glasses and got up from her chair, and Lisa and Marc sat down on it next to the knitting stuff. The two of them sailed across the room, leaving a trail of unraveling blue yarn. The lady waved the one knitting needle she still had and shouted, "HELP!"

There were two other people in the rec room. They were so surprised that they just stood and watched and fluttered their hands. We made a hasty exit out the art room window, then ran back to the pool—on the grass—and kicked the KEEP OFF sign again. Paul went over to the poolside radio that usually played "Golden Oldies." He turned the dial until he got pure static. "That's all we get around here, anyway!" he shouted.

At the deep end of the pool we stood right on the words NO DIVING. Luckily for them and us, Grandma and Grandpa were still upstairs, and there were only about five people around. Marc and I cracked our knuckles at the same time, then we all let out

earsplitting yells and dove directly into the pool—all four of us, no bathing caps, no showers, nothing! We made a gigantic splash that sent a wave of water over the pool edge. When we came up to the surface all five adults were soaked and speechless.

# 5
# OVERREACTION

---

Dear Mom and Dad,

Who are these people living in Grandma
and Grandpa's bodies? Having a miserable
time. Wish you were here. That doesn't
sound right but you will know what I mean.

> Love and tears,
> Stacy (& Marc)

P.S. Sorry I didn't mail a card yesterday. I
was so mad I ripped it up.

---

The morning of day six I really felt low thinking about
yesterday's rec room riot. But what I couldn't understand was that even though I felt bad about that woman's knitting getting wrecked and those five people at
the pool getting soaked, I wasn't sorry I'd ridden
around on those rec room couches. I felt mixed-up,
like a dumped-out jigsaw puzzle. I hadn't slept much,
worrying about the rebellion and how to tell Grandma
and Grandpa about it. I kept on wondering what they

would say when they found out what their own grandchildren had done. I wondered if Grandma and
Grandpa would still love me, the real me, the one
that's not perfect.

No one had complained yet. Maybe they'd all been
in such a rush to get to the early bird dinners last
night, they didn't take time out even for that. And
Marc and I hadn't told Grandma and Grandpa last
night, first, because we didn't want to spoil the
Chanukah celebration. Marc lit the shammes and I lit
four candles; Grandpa said our gift tonight couldn't
be wrapped.

The second reason for not telling was the Chanukah
gift itself. It turned out to be Reggie and Joe taking us
out for hamburgers and then to an ice skating rink.
They'd asked Lisa and Paul to go, too, but they had to
go to dinner with their grandparents. I wished they'd
been able to go with us . . . especially Paul. Maybe
we would have skated double or something.

"Hurry up. Get ready," Grandma had said. "Go ice
skating with Reggie and Joe. It's also a gift for them.
They miss their own grandchildren so much, it'll do
them good. And they do so many nice things for other
people. I forget exactly where, but they go to this
place and help out a few days a week."

"Monday, Wednesday, and Friday?" I asked.

"Something like that," she said. "They mentioned it
at the pool once, but everyone there was talking at the
same time. Who can hear? Go. Don't keep them waiting. And wear a sweater or you'll get a chill."

"Herb called to see if we could use his tickets to
*Camelot* at the Parker Playhouse tonight," Grandpa

explained. "He had to fly to Washington for a Gray Panthers protest."

So Grandma and Grandpa drove off in one direction, and Reggie and Joe, Marc and I went off in another.

We had a great time. Reggie and Joe skated too. And it was neat to ice skate indoors and then go outside and have it be summer weather. If Reggie and Joe knew about the rec room wreck, they sure kept it a secret.

When we got home Grandma and Grandpa were already in bed. They just called out to us, "Good night, kids. We're exhausted. See you in the morning. I left out cookies if you want some." Grandma added, "Be careful of crumbs. We don't need ants."

I couldn't eat cookies. I couldn't even sleep. I kept thinking of Grandma and Grandpa finding out about our rebellion. Marc can always sleep, even when he has finals—but I kept tossing and turning. Finally I put on my robe and took a newspaper into the bathroom. I figured I'd sit there and look at the ads to take my mind off my worrying. Except these ads didn't help.

Now I'd seen everything: a do-it-yourself funeral kit? I turned the page. There was another funeral ad.

This one was really strange. It had a picture of a boat, but the words said

and they gave the phone number.

What were they going to do, toss the bodies overboard? These ads were getting gross, and they were not the answers to *my* problem. Sure my grandparents might kill me when I told them what we'd done, but kill me, like punish, not kill me, like dead and overboard or whatever. Still, the ads were so weird I ripped them out to show to Marc. Then I went back to bed.

It was beginning to get light out when I figured out something important. These past five days I'd been expecting Grandma and Grandpa to be mind readers, to know what Marc and I wanted to do when we didn't even ask them. I decided that after breakfast I'd definitely tell my grandparents my feelings—and explain the rebellion. I wouldn't put it off again. But I wasn't ready for what happened next. I never thought there would be open warfare. Talk about overreaction —the sixth day was unbelievable!

When we woke up Grandma was in her bathing suit on the terrace sipping coffee. The coffee smell was strong.

"Grandpa's been called to an emergency meeting of the men's club," she said. "Someone even came and got him. And I have to go to an emergency meeting of the women's club as soon as possible," she added, brushing toast crumbs from the table into her hand. "This is such an emergency that the two groups are even meeting together. It must be about the rec lease again. Buying it so we don't have to pay to use what we all thought we owned."

Marc and I looked at each other and cracked our knuckles. I didn't think the meeting was about the rec room lease.

Grandma left before we could say a word. "Meet us at the pool," she called over her shoulder, "after you eat your cornflakes and milk. I already poured it into the bowls. Don't let it get soggy." She stopped to pick up a thread or something that stuck to the yellow carpet.

Who could eat? Marc and I pushed the cornflakes around with our spoons for a while, and finally we just dumped them into the sink. Then we started to straighten up the room.

"Stacy." Marc cleared his throat and spoke softly as he made the bed. "Do you think we're the emergency?"

"We're the emergency, all right. No doubt about it. We should have told them ourselves."

"I was going to tell them this morning," Marc said, and he pounded the pillow angrily before he put it up in the closet.

"I was, too," I said. "I was going to tell them last night, but first we were rushed off to ice skate with Reggie and Joe and then by the time we were all home Grandpa and Grandma were in bed."

We put on our bathing suits and walked to the elevator very slowly. I mailed the postcard in the mailbox near the elevator, then we went on to the pool. We passed a man digging in his garden. It was between two cement areas, only about two-by-two, but it was full of flowers, and the man was carefully watering each one.

"That's a nice garden," I told him. He looked up squinting and said, "It passes the time."

By the time we got to the pool the meeting must have been over because Ted, wearing matching yellow pants and shirt, was tacking up new rules signs. I noticed his shoes were white patent leather. I wondered if I was getting like Grandma and Grandpa, noticing shoes all the time. I wished they'd stop doing that.

As Lisa and Paul walked over to us a car pulled up and a horn beeped.

"Paul, here is the key. Have a wonderful day, love. We'll be over there." Paul's grandmother pointed up the road at the condominium's golf course. "We're only playing nine holes."

Paul's grandfather added, "Lisa, you listen to your brother, okay?"

Paul took the key his grandmother dangled out the car window. Then the car zoomed off with a last honk of the horn. Paul walked back to where I stood reading one of the signs.

CHILDREN UNDER 18 ARE NOT PERMITTED TO LOITER IN POOL OR RECREATION AREAS.

I could feel this vein in the side of my forehead throbbing as I got angrier and angrier. Just then the

Lemon Cove bike riders passed by, yellow T-shirts and all. A woman with her hair up in rollers rode a tricycle with a wire basket in front. They all had red and yellow streamers in their bike wheels, and they greeted Ted noisily with their horns and bells. Ted waved back and shouted, "Everything's under control!"

I poked Marc. "How come no one tells them they're making too much noise? I bet if we did that they'd have a fit."

"I bet if we did that they'd consider us a motorcycle gang," Paul added. He stood close to me and put his hands on my shoulders to move me a bit so he could read the new rules sign again. Only he didn't move his hands off my shoulders—and I noticed that I didn't want him to.

More and more people gathered at the pool till there must have been about fifty. It sounded like a beehive—everyone seemed to be talking at the same time. Some kids started over toward us, but their grandparents gave us a nasty look, pulled them back, and handed them a Monopoly set. Next thing I knew a policeman arrived, gun, nightstick, and all. It made me angrier than ever.

"What are they going to do? Arrest all the grand-children?" I said to Paul. I poked my finger like a gun at Marc, Paul, and Lisa, and said, "Put your hands up. You're under arrest. You destroyed the peace."

"He's not a real policeman," Paul whispered in my ear. "He's a security guard. See the patch on his shoulder?"

The guard loomed above us, suntanned and gray-haired. "You committed a nuisance in the rec room," he said, looking me right in the eye.

I stopped pointing my finger and cracked my knuckles instead. Then the worst thing happened. I just started laughing. I couldn't stop myself. Maybe it was because I was nervous. What he had said sounded like one of the signs about curbing your dog, or a TV ad for a pooper-scooper. I repeated his words, "Committed a nuisance in the rec room?" I knew Marc was biting his lip so he wouldn't start laughing, too. Once it gets started, there is no controlling that kind of giggling attack.

Then Lisa began to laugh. "What am I laughing at?" she sputtered and laughed some more. Only Paul still controlled himself.

"Animals!" I heard the woman with the crooked toes say.

That did it. Paul doubled over, and we all laughed the kind of laugh that bursts out because you're trying so hard to hold it in. We snorted. We choked. We coughed and sputtered. My eyes teared and I could hardly see. But they were not tears of regret.

"That's the trouble with you young people," a heavyset man with a cigar mumbled. "Everything's a big joke."

"Just wait till your grandparents get down to the pool," this man with a beard said to me.

Ted glared at us like a hawk waiting to attack. "This officer will be in charge." He looked at the security guard with respect and added, "We are paying him." What *were* my grandparents going to do?

66

"All our rules are to be obeyed," Ted went on, "or else we will take the necessary actions." He nodded toward the security guard. "So you better watch it!" He seemed to spit out the last words.

The woman with white stuff on her nose said, "You want to sit and enjoy an afternoon at the pool, and there's no chairs because of the grandchildren."

Marc pointed to another kid sitting on one of the chairs. He was pulling threads from his towel and winding them around his finger. "You can't win around here. Even if you sit down, you're in trouble at this place," Marc said.

"*Especially* if you sit down on the pool steps," Lisa added.

If there was lightning they'd probably blame that on us grandchildren, too, I thought as I watched a woman tack up another rules sign: CHAIRS AND LOUNGES FOR RESIDENTS ONLY *NOT GUESTS*.

I whispered to Paul, "Why can't they just say PLEASE BRING EXTRA CHAIRS?"

"They write everything so it sounds mean," he whispered back. "Even my own grandparents left early this morning to jog and wrote us a note that said TAKE BREAKFAST AND CLEAN UP. They never were the kind of grandparents who took us places, but they used to play with us sometimes."

"Usually I act the meanest when I feel like things are unfair," I said, "like when my mom or dad says you never help and I just straightened the food closet only they didn't look yet." I remembered thinking about that at dinner with Herb the other night when

67

he was talking about the Gray Panthers fighting unfairness to older people. We could sure use Herb around here. I wished Grandma and Grandpa would join the Gray Panthers. Then maybe they'd understand our rebellion. "I wonder if the people retired here feel that something is unfair," I added.

Paul stood next to me and listened. "I'm no shrink," he said, "but if you ask me, they have the same expression as my cat has when she's been in her carrying case."

I have to admit I wasn't happy with the way I'd acted in the rec room. That is not the kind of kid I am. In my class yearbook it says I'm the kid that is most responsible. But something here at Lemon Cove was bringing out the worst in me. Except that I wasn't the only one that was happening to.

Grandma and Grandpa and Reggie came walking slowly down the road and joined us. But Joe walked on the grass. Grandpa looked angry. Only instead of yelling at us, he yelled at Ted.

"What do you mean by calling the authorities?" he said. "You have trouble with my grandchildren, you call me, not a guard, and you give me a chance to handle it! You did not have my approval to spend a single penny on this foolishness. *You* did not follow the rules!"

I smiled at Grandpa, proud that he'd spoken up at last. He did not smile back. "You, I'll talk to later," he said, waving his finger.

Ted, with his hands on his hips and his nose in the air, said, "Why can't your grandchildren obey the rules like those other kids?" He pointed to the kids with the Monopoly set and the bored looks. But he also yelled at them, "Be careful. That Monopoly money will fly away and litter. Why can't you control your grandchildren, Mr. Zimmerman?"

Grandpa didn't have a chance to answer because there was suddenly a big splash in the pool. I couldn't believe my eyes. Marc, Lisa, Paul, and I watched for the head to come up. It was Joe. After surfacing from his dive, he swam across the pool with his gray hair dripping and his feet kicking so hard they made the water foam. Reggie and Grandma walked to the pool steps and sat down with what my mother calls "a defiant look" at Ted.

"If I knew how to dive, I would," Reggie said.

"Me, too," Grandma said, adding, "if I didn't just have my hair done"—she patted her hair—"I'd dive in, too."

Grandma's hair looked nice, but her eyes looked even nicer. They were sparkling.

I felt so proud of my grandparents and Reggie. But I still knew our problems were not over yet. Grandpa's waving finger had told me that.

# 6
# WHAT NEXT!

The ripples in the pool calmed as Joe climbed up the
ladder, the one he'd fixed. Grandma and Reggie got
up and walked to where Joe was hopping on one foot
shaking water out of his ears. I raced over to them and
hugged first Grandma, then Reggie, then Joe. Most of
the other adults were mumbling angrily, but for once
Ted was speechless.

"Troublemakers," said the woman with the white
ointment on her lips. Her accusing look now included
Joe, for his diving, and Reggie and Grandma for their
pool steps sit-in. The other kids around the pool were
considered troublemakers, too, even though they
weren't really in the rec room riot. Around here,
being young was reason enough to be included. People were even looking at Grandpa suspiciously.

"So we don't need a guard, huh, Mr. Zimmerman?"
the man with the hairy chest said sarcastically.

"I wonder what my grandparents will say when
they find out about the riot," Paul whispered to me.
"Maybe they won't stay in one place long enough to
find out."

"They'll find out later," Lisa said, "when they go

play cards in the sewing room. Every room in the clubhouse seems to be a cardroom, no matter what it says on the door," Lisa added, twisting strands of her blond hair.

"Let's go up to the apartment," Grandpa ordered. "Right now!"

"See you later," I said to Paul and Lisa. I had to take giant steps to catch up to Grandma and Grandpa and the Feldmans. I tugged at Marc's hand and we ran to the elevator, to the background tune of "Don't run!"

We didn't get away with what we'd done, but we didn't want to get away with it. Sometimes if I've done something mean I feel better if someone punishes me. So I was glad when, on the way up in the elevator, Grandpa took charge.

"Since I am the only one who controlled myself, in actions, anyway, I'll have to be the one to make you pay for your outbursts and splashes," he said. He had trouble keeping a straight face as he included Joe, Reggie, and Grandma in his announcement.

"No television for a week," I suggested, but Grandpa was too smart for that.

"Joe and Reggie don't watch TV," Grandpa said as we got out on the third floor. "And this is no joking matter," he added. I noticed his eyes twinkled with an old Brooklyn look, an angry one but still a *Brooklyn* one, like when someone pulled into the parking spot he'd been waiting for and he got them to pull out.

"No allowance," Marc said dramatically, as if it was a real sacrifice.

"Joe and Reggie and Grandma get their allowance

71

from the government," Grandpa explained. "Social Security, it's called. And you and Stacy got your allowance in advance, for spending money, didn't you?"

Grandpa squinted his eyes trying to look tough, but it didn't work. We walked down the catwalk, silent except for the slapping sound of Grandma's slippers. She walked with determination, like she used to in the shoe store when she'd said to a customer, "I know just the right shoe for you."

Physical punishment was out. Grandpa was nonviolent. We were in front of Reggie and Joe's apartment when Grandpa got the idea to send us all to our rooms. "Let's all give this punishment problem some thought while we change out of our bathing suits and rest," Grandpa said. "After dinner let's meet at our apartment and discuss the situation further over dessert."

"See you later," Reggie called as she and Joe went inside. "We have to rush. Because of that emergency meeting, we're late already." I wanted to ask what they were late for, but they had disappeared inside.

"Invite your friends Lisa and Paul, too," Grandpa said as we walked to our apartment. "And their grandparents as well," he added, unlocking the door. He and Grandma went right to their room and closed the door.

I figured we were in for a speech tonight for sure. I dialed the kitchen phone kind of hoping I'd hear Paul's voice, but Lisa answered.

"Paul's in the shower," she said, "and then we have to go out for dinner when our grandparents get back from shuffleboard. But we could come over for dessert

72

if our grandparents don't kill us first," she added. "Wasn't Joe super!" she said, and her voice sounded like a giggle.

"Yeah. And Reggie and my grandma did okay, too," I added before we said good-bye.

I got dressed fast, and while I waited on the terrace for Marc, I clipped another ad from the newspaper. Maybe I noticed it now because I felt like I was sitting on pins and needles, but I had never seen an ad for an "acupuncture open house" before.

ACUPUNCTURE OPEN HOUSE
SUNDAY 10–4
CENTER FOR ARTHRITIC STUDY—UNIVERSITY AVE.
FREE DEMONSTRATION AND COFFEE AND CAKE

Maybe we could donate Ted and cure his arthritis and bad temper. I stuffed the ad into my pocket.

At sundown I set up the five Chanukah candles, plus the shammes lighting candle, each candle a beautiful pastel color. When everyone was ready we said the blessing, first in Hebrew then in English, and lit the candles. We were so quiet, it made unwrapping our presents sound noisy. Tonight's Chanukah presents were puzzle books, one for Marc and one for me. "To keep you busy," Grandpa said. "But if I'd known what you had in mind yesterday, I might have gotten you handcuffs." He was trying hard to sound tough. But I guess it wasn't working if it showed that he was just trying.

"Stacy and I love crosswords," Marc said. Except I knew how he hated puzzles.

73

Later, when I tried to talk during dinner, Grandpa said, "You're supposed to be thinking and eating. Talk we'll do later when everyone's here."

The silent treatment is awful. It makes me have so much to say. Here we were together on the terrace, watching the candles melt and eating dinner, our first at-home, Grandma-cooked meal, and all I could do was push green peas and broiled chicken around on my plate. A gentle breeze brushed my shoulders and a duck in the canal below splashed and flapped its wings. The candles flickered and the flames almost went out, but they didn't—not till they just disappeared along with the candles, leaving curls of smoke in the air.

At 7:30 the doorbell rang, and Joe and Reggie came in and sat down opposite me at the table. They were chatting about this and that, but Grandpa was still silent.

Grandma got up to fix the dessert, saying, "Sit, all of you. I'll just be a few minutes."

The doorbell rang again, and Grandpa let Paul and Lisa in—alone.

"Our grandparents don't believe us," Paul muttered as he sat down next to me at the terrace table, across from Joe. "They either don't hear us or don't listen anymore. They hear us if we make the slightest noise, so I know their hearing is all right. We told them what we did. All they said was, 'You have to taste the homebaked bread in this restaurant. It melts in your mouth.' Then, as if there were other people at the table, my grandmother said, 'Our grandchildren don't do such things. And if they did, it's because of the

75

bad influence of someone else's ill-mannered grandchildren. Pass the butter, please.'" Paul gave a good imitation, but he wasn't joking. It hurt him to see that his grandparents had changed so. Joe could tell, too. He reached out and patted Paul's arm.

"They wouldn't come here tonight. They had invited friends over," Lisa said.

"They'll come another time," Grandma soothed as she served dessert. It was chocolate pudding, the kind you cook and burn your tongue on licking the spoon —real chocolate pudding. "And what lovely sandals you're wearing, Lisa," Grandma added as she almost tripped over Lisa's foot. Again it made me sad when she said that as if she were still in the shoe business. It's like the feeling I get when I wish I was back in grade school instead of junior high.

"Thanks," Lisa said, pulling her foot in. Then she went on. "Each year they're here, my grandparents seem to care less about us and more about themselves and their friends and their card games and bingo."

"Getting the right table to play cards at is the most important thing in the world to them," Paul interrupted.

"They never spent a lot of time with us, like you spend with Stacy and Marc," Lisa went on, looking as if she might cry. "But now it's like we're invisible altogether. At least they used to be in the same room with us, even if they were reading or listening to music, and if we asked them about the songs they'd explain things."

"It's not easy for kids down here," Reggie sighed.

Joe reached over and held Reggie's hand. "I wish our grandchildren would give it another try. I'd understand this time."

I helped Grandma serve coffee to the adults and milk to us kids.

Grandpa cleared his throat. "Now let's get down to business. So did it help? The problem is solved? A rec room riot? A hippie, sit-in-on-the-pool-steps-grandma we have here now. Disobeying rules and diving in the pool solves problems?" Grandpa glared at Paul, Marc, Lisa, and me, and at Grandma and Reggie and Joe, too. His blue eyes penetrated right into your brain cells. I had to speak up.

"But it did help, Grandpa, in a way," I said. I took a gulp of cool milk and wiped my mouth with a napkin so I wouldn't have a milk mustache. I don't care about that at home, but with Paul here, well, it was different. "It helped because at least everyone's feelings are out in the open now. We're not all angry inside," I explained.

"Not the best way, though, Stacy," Grandpa said. "But unfortunately maybe it had to be that way." He scratched his head. "Still, pushing the rules in their faces doesn't change anything. Two wrongs don't make a right."

My father always says that. Thinking of my father made me wish I had activated my brain first and stopped the rebellion a little sooner, before we had upset the woman with the knitting. But she was so nasty. I still wasn't really sorry.

"Maybe we did two rights that only look wrong?"

Grandma said, stirring her coffee and watching the ripples the spoon made in the cup. Grandma was giving answers but saying them as if they were questions. Like in Brooklyn. "Maybe we should just pretend nothing happened?"

"Sometimes," Reggie added, "you have to do something a little bit wrong to make something very wrong a little bit better. The heck with the pool and all its rules. I prefer the ocean anyway."

"What we don't need now is philosophy," Grandpa interrupted. "What we do need are solutions. We still want to swim at the pool. We can't always make trouble." Grandpa drummed his fingers on the glass table-top.

Joe was very quiet. He just listened and kept folding his paper napkin into smaller and smaller squares.

"This is really a tough problem," Paul admitted. "A lot of the rules don't make sense. The way a lot of the people act toward kids doesn't make sense. But I guess a lot of what we did in the rec room didn't make sense, either—but the reason we did it does. It seems like everybody's right and yet everybody's wrong."

"And I'm still not wearing a bathing cap," Marc added. "This conversation is sure ruining the taste of some good chocolate pudding." I wanted to come up with a brilliant solution. But so many feelings were inside me that there seemed to be no room for ideas.

"You know," Grandpa finally said, "the best thing we could do for the residents of Lemon Cove would be to let them have a day without us."

"Can Paul and I go with you," Lisa asked, "wherever you're going?"

"Of course," Grandma said, "you're always welcome." She brushed a long blond hair away from Lisa's eyes.

"We could all use a day to cool off," Marc said, reaching for another chocolate pudding.

"How many is that?" Grandma asked. "More than two chocolate puddings equals a bellyache."

"A day away to cool off and come up with a solution," Grandpa said sternly, pointing a finger at us all in turn. I noticed he had gray hairs growing on his fingers. Older people seem to have a lot of hair. Maybe it's not on their heads, but so what.

Joe finally spoke. "I think I have the best idea," he said, leaning forward, arms on the table. "We could spend the day away from Lemon Cove and do something helpful at the same time."

"Like what?" I asked, sitting up straight in my chair.

"You could all just come with Reggie and me. We can go again tomorrow and skip Friday, that's what we'll do," he said to Reggie.

"Sure," said Reggie. "It's a flexible schedule there."

"Where?" I asked, eager to know where the Feldmans went three days a week.

"We'll take you all to the Center for the Blind," Joe said. "Reggie and I work there as volunteers, usually on Monday, Wednesday, and Friday."

"Sure," Reggie agreed, "they could all come with us." She turned to Grandma, who was starting to clear the table. "I'd love to show you that place."

79

It would be nice to do something for someone else, I thought. But this was a vacation. I still would rather swim, even if it was in the ocean and not in the pool. Or at least we could play tennis. I almost disagreed out loud, but then I remembered I'd be with Paul all day.

"It might help to find a reasonable plan to ease this condominium crisis if we're away from this unreasonable place," Grandpa said, turning to Lisa and Paul. "Will you kids be able to go? Maybe your grandparents would like to go, too?"

"Our grandparents are in a bridge tournament tomorrow. They won't care if we're away," Lisa said. Her voice was sad again. "But I'm sure they wouldn't go with us."

I had to squeeze by Paul as I got up to help Grandma clear the table. I was sure I'd remember forever exactly how it felt to touch him. It made me like him even more when he helped clear the table with us, even though all he'd had was chocolate pudding. I thought of brushing my hair two hundred strokes. Maybe if I was prettier—then I bet Paul would notice me.

When the dishes were done, Joe and Reggie said, "Over and out," and left to walk Paul and Lisa home, saying they sure missed their own grandchildren and wished they'd come to visit again.

Marc and I watched TV along with Grandma and Grandpa in their big king-size bed. We always used to do that in Brooklyn. Later, as I was trying to fall asleep, I wondered if blind people dream and if they see in their dreams. It was real dark in the room and I wondered what it was like not to be able to see. Do blind people worry about what they look like? Would I say the right thing tomorrow or would I say or do something stupid? I felt a little scared but I was also exhausted.

We all met in the parking lot at nine in the morning of day seven. About a dozen people in Lemon Cove sweat shirts jogged by. The people here look like they even iron their sweat shirts.

It was a beautiful swimming day, but by now I was more curious to see Joe and Reggie in action at the Center for the Blind, and I would not miss Ted, the pool captain, one bit. I thought about giving him the acupuncture ad to cure his arthritis and bad temper but I was chicken. Besides, I had more important things to think about, like Paul.

I'd tried to look as pretty as I could today, so maybe Paul would like me. I mean really like me. My jeans were imitation designer label and in my back pocket I had a comb that I used on my shaggy hair every five minutes. It was a yellow comb that matched the color of my tube top, and where the comb stuck out of my pocket it had the words CURVES AHEAD. I wished it said CURVES AHEAD SOON.

As we got into Joe's station wagon, I watched to see if Paul was going to sit in the back seat with Grandma and Grandpa or on the back station wagon platform with Lisa and Marc. He chose the platform, got in, and stretched his legs. I got in next to him. But he didn't really notice. We started off.

Marc and Lisa both had their eyes closed. "What's

that buzzing sound?" Marc asked, pretending to be blind. "A moped going by?"

"I think so," Lisa said, her eyes tightly shut. "I smell the exhaust from it, too. My father takes me for rides on his motorcycle. It smells like that."

An ambulance passed by, siren blaring. "That's the Florida symphony," Grandpa said. "You hear sirens day and night."

"Don't they make you nervous?" I asked.

"No," he answered. "When you're our age, the sound of sirens nearby makes you feel safe. In case you need them, you know they're there."

"What's that clicking noise?" Lisa asked, getting back to the guessing game. I knew it was Paul clicking one fingernail against another. He seemed as nervous as I was about meeting blind people.

"What do we do there, Joe?" he asked. "What if we do something wrong?"

"We help the clients off the bus and serve them juice and coffee to begin with," Joe said. "We lead them to the tables. If you do something wrong, they'll tell you, that's all."

The thought of doing something wrong still scared me.

"Some of the people have partial sight," Reggie added, turning around to look at us, "and others are totally blind."

"Wait till you meet Doc Levinson. He runs the place," Joe said, all smiles. Reggie was smiling, too.

"When you open a door for a blind person," Joe instructed, "if it opens to the right, hold it with your left hand and lead the person. If it opens the other way tell the client—blind people at the Center are called clients, and we're called volunteers."

Grandma and Grandpa were listening closely.

"Why didn't you ever tell us more about your work at the Center for the Blind?" Grandpa asked Reggie and Joe. "It's so interesting to listen to you."

"I once started to, but people at the Lemon Cove pool talk all at once. No one really listens," Joe said, glancing in the rearview mirror. "All they're interested in is who's in the wrong parking spot and making rules. So I don't talk about the Center for the Blind, or anything else that means something to me. I just find something around the pool that needs fixing —and I fix it."

I knew what he meant. I keep a lot to myself, too. No one knows about all the things I clip and save or the sketches I make now and then.

We drove to Seventh Avenue and waited as North River Bridge went up to let a sailboat go by. Joe pointed to a white building across the water. "That's it," he said. "The Center's on the ground floor of that housing project. And you're going to meet your match in playing horseshoes," Joe said to Grandpa.

"Horseshoes they play? Without seeing?" Grandma asked.

"Sure," Reggie piped in, "they listen for the metal sound of the horseshoe hitting the post. A volunteer tells them where to throw it. If they hear the sound they know they hit the peg."

Joe parked the car and we got out. I was scared yet excited to go inside, and I tried to imagine what it would look like. I wondered if blind people do that, try to picture something they've never seen.

"I can't wait to get to work," Grandpa said as we followed Joe. I think Grandpa and I were both interested in what it would be like inside.

# 7
# TIME OUT

We walked up the path and into the lobby of Boatway Condominiums, where people from the housing project were crowded around the mailboxes. They looked excited, as if something special was happening.

"Mailman's coming," Grandpa explained, pointing to a jolly, Santa-like man wearing shorts. He wore long black socks at one end and a jungle helmet at the other. The people watcher in me was very busy. I figured I might want to make a sketch of him.

"Today's the day the Social Security checks come. The folks at Lemon Cove are probably waiting at the mailboxes, too," Grandpa said.

I could smell the leather from the mailbag.

"I think the mailperson's the most important person in Florida," Joe said. "Anything that's important, he brings: letters from family, checks, birthday cards. Helmet protects him from the sun."

"How come the people at the pool don't wear helmets?" Lisa asked, but she didn't wait for an answer. She raced ahead. Lisa has this graceful look, like a dancer or a gymnast. She almost seems to fly.

"Come on," Joe called over his shoulder. Like first

graders out on a nature trip, the rest of us followed him single file past the crowd of people.

"The air conditioning doesn't work too well in here," Joe explained. His gray hair was blown around as we entered a wood-paneled room with whirring fans on the ceiling. There was a Christmas tree in one corner. I smelled the pine needles and was glad it wasn't a palm plant. Next to the tree was an electric Chanukah menorah with its shammes candle lit, plus five electric candles glowing just like in our grandparents' apartment last night. I was happy to see both kinds of decorations. Maybe you don't have to see holiday lights to enjoy them. Even blind people must feel happy as they put them up.

"There he is! There's Doc Levinson. Hey, Doc," Joe shouted to a gray-haired man who was adjusting a microphone. "Here are the new volunteers I told you about on the phone."

Doc Levinson walked over to us and Reggie introduced us to him. What really surprised me was that this Doc Levinson, this director who runs everything, was about seventy-five years old, kind of rugged looking—like a sailor—and blind.

"Welcome to the Center," he said, shaking our hands. "We'll keep you hopping around here. We can always use some extra eyes. Now we'd better get ready. If you brought the ingredients for the cookie-making class Joe asked me about on the phone," he said to Grandma, "you can put everything in the kitchen." He motioned to a nearby doorway. "Help yourself to the pans and stuff," he told her. "Make yourself at home. Yell if you need help."

"I've got everything I'll need," Grandma said. "I'll just rummage around in these cabinets for the cookie sheets. Don't worry about me one bit."

"That's the kind of volunteer we need around here," Doc Levinson said, patting Grandma on the back. Then he led us back to the main room.

I laughed to myself as I heard Grandma say, "Now if I was a cookie sheet, where would I be?" Back in Brooklyn she used to talk like that when she was trying to find a certain box of shoes. "If I were girls' black patent leather Mary Janes, size one, where would I be?" she used to say.

"Take the chairs off the tables," Doc Levinson instructed, "and put them around each table. Put out the sugar and milk. The buses will be here in five minutes."

"Kids, you do the tables and chairs," Grandpa said to us. "I'll take care of the milk and sugar."

We all got busy.

"In the evening this room is a rec hall for the residents," Reggie explained, as she unrolled the mats for her yoga class.

"You mean a Florida rec room and we're allowed in it? An all-time first." Marc was beginning to sound as sarcastic as Lisa.

"Poor Ted, the pool captain." Marc pretended to wipe away a tear. "Today he'll really have nothing to do."

"We won't be there for him to scream at," Lisa added and wiped away her own make-believe tear.

I wondered if blind people cry tears. Paul must

have been wondering about things, too. He was very quiet. He just looked around at everything.

"Isn't that Doc Levinson something?" Joe whispered. "A fantastic man. He's a retired physicist. Lost an eye playing ball at age thirteen, and fourteen years ago he lost vision in his other eye. Instead of pitying himself he decided to help other blind people."

When he was my age he lost an eye? I got a chill.

We put eight chairs at each table, arranging them on the linoleum floor. I was glad Joe had explained how Doc Levinson got blind. I'm curious about things like that.

"The buses!" Doc Levinson shouted, and we all followed his tapping cane.

I was so nervous I stepped on Paul's foot. I think I turned a brilliant shade called "embarrassed red." That was not exactly the way I'd wanted Paul to notice me. I waited for Paul to say something like "Boy, are you clumsy" or "Have a nice trip? See you next fall."

He just smiled and said, "I step on them myself."

Three buses pulled in with a smell of hot exhaust fumes, and we helped the people step off.

"Sorry," this short bald man said as his cane tapped my leg.

"That's okay," I answered.

"Who is it?" a gray, curly-haired woman called to me. She wore bright red lipstick, a little smudged on her top lip, and glasses with thick lenses. She had partial sight.

"I'm a volunteer," I said and it sounded so important. "I'm Stacy."

"Come over when we do knitting and I'll show you a sweater I'm making. I'm Belle. You sound young. I'll have to clean up my jokes a little," she laughed.

"I'll look forward to being there," I called and then bit my lip. Why on earth did I have to say "look"? I had the feeling my color of the day was beet red. But Belle didn't seem to notice what I'd said. She was inside now, busy helping this blond-haired man find the sugar for his coffee.

"Do I hear Reggie and Joe?" a new voice called over the conversation and the clink of coffee cups and spoons.

"Yup, you do. We're over here, Marty," Joe called from the next table.

"Keep talking and I'll find you," Marty said. Joe kept talking until Marty was with him.

Marty looked about twenty-eight, and very handsome and well dressed. He was wearing an expensive-looking silk shirt and white pants. He took Joe's hand and began running his fingers over a wooden board, as if he was teaching Joe something.

Joe called Grandma, Grandpa, Marc, Lisa, Paul, and me over to watch. "Marty's teaching me Braille," he explained. "Someday I'm going to teach Braille, too." That's what I loved about Joe—his "somedays." He didn't just do things like that man in his garden— "to pass time"—or just talk about "Used to be's."

After coffee the place was humming. I could almost feel the activity in my braces. "Everything looks so interesting to me," I said to Paul. "See, there, I said it again. 'Look' and 'see' are my words of the day. I never realized how often I said them."

"I guess we're all used to saying things that way," Paul said, "because we *do* see."

I tugged Paul's hand and pulled him toward Belle's knitting group, which was laughing hysterically at her jokes. And the jokes were dirty, all right. We moved on to the ceramics group. All around were busy sounds: the tapping of canes, the public address system with Doc Levinson announcing activities and reading a list of new Braille books and tapes. And the hum of a spinning potter's wheel.

Across the room Reggie was teaching yoga, and next to us Joe was leading a terrific discussion group on current events. Some people said "I hear you!" instead of "I see" when they understood. After the news items Joe read the ads for bargain specials. "Tuna's on special at the Winn Dixie supermarket," he said and turned the page of the newspaper.

"Otherwise the clients wouldn't know about specials, would they?" Paul whispered to me. "I never thought about that."

"Me either," I said.

I loved one ad Joe had clipped from another paper. It was a suggested Christmas gift certificate to Publix supermarkets. So Joe was a newspaper clipper like me.

Grandma called me from the nearby kitchen, where she was busy teaching cookie making. I went to see if she needed help, and Paul came with me. "Look what I'm doing," she said happily. "I can make these choco-late chocolate-chip cookies with my eyes shut," Grandma said to the clients, "so I'm sure you can make them as well." Grandma's words embarrassed me, and I looked at Paul, sort of trying to make an excuse for her. But the clients laughed. They were enjoying themselves, and Grandma.

"It's okay, Stacy, you and Paul can go. I just wanted to show you how I can manage," Grandma said, handing out wooden mixing spoons and bowls to the clients.

We walked back into the main room, where Doc Levinson suggested we choose a craft group to work with.

I could hear Grandpa, in the corner at the desk, making phone calls to clients who hadn't come, to see if they needed a ride or were sick or something. His voice sounded real friendly. "Yallo," he said, and I laughed—I can always tell it's Grandpa on the phone because he always says "Yallo" instead of "Hello."

"We're taking this group out to play basketball," Lisa and Marc called from the doorway. "They have this special basketball you can hear. It beeps!" Marc added. "Doc Levinson's gonna be with us."

"Sounds like fun!" I called as they went out.

I was beginning to wonder if Paul was following me or I was following him. Everything was going so well. Maybe he was beginning to notice me. I was glad I'd shampooed my hair and extra conditioned it.

Paul and I helped an older girl, Beth, who was teaching a group how to make decorated tiles. She was blind but she wasn't a client. Joe had told me she was a paid instructor.

The clients in our ceramic group smelled the cookies baking in the kitchen even before I did, and I thought I had the most sensitive nose in the world.

"Boy, does that smell good," a man said. "Hope we get samples."

"You'll get, you'll get," Grandma said as she and her group came out of the kitchen. Grandma was wiping her forehead with a tissue. "It's like an oven in there. We came out for a breath of air while the cookies are baking."

One client, Tom, must have liked doing tiles a lot. He was putting extra ones in his pockets. Kind of like the kids who sneak extra plastic in shop. I guess he figured no one could see.

"Isn't that Beth really something?" I whispered to Paul, and he nodded. Besides being blind, she also had half of one leg missing. She wore a skirt, but I could see where the artificial leg joined her own leg—a piece of gauze didn't quite hide it.

This other young man, Marty, sure liked her a lot. They'd laugh together, and when they touched hands they held on for a while. Marty couldn't know if she was pretty or ugly.

I looked at Paul and probably turned red, because he was looking at me. But this wasn't the kind of look that noticed if your hair was combed or if you had the latest grape lip gloss on. My hand got shaky and I almost messed up the ceramic figure I was painting. Something was happening to me, except I wasn't sure what it was. But everything was going great—until the thing I'd dreaded the most happened.

A young client, Ellen, was carrying a tray of tiles and I could see she was going to bump into this other guy. So I jumped up and put my hands on her shoulders, trying to lead her. She turned suddenly, kind of pushing at me with her shoulder. She practically knocked me over. Then she threw out her hands, and the tiles went flying. I'd only wanted to help. I got so scared. And so embarrassed.

"I'm not a piece of luggage, you know!" she yelled. "Don't ever push me!"

I couldn't hold back my tears. "I'm sorry," I said to Ellen. "I just wanted to help."

Ellen took my hand and said just what I'd said to myself yesterday, about Grandma and Grandpa and me. "I'm sorry," she said. "You can't expect people to know how you feel without telling them. I can't stand being thought of as 'blind' instead of as Ellen! Let me show you the right way to lead a person who can't see. You take the person's left hand and put it under your right arm, and you walk along together like this." And Ellen and I walked along. "You never push," she explained. "It startled me when you did that. I got angry because I was clumsy. I guess I feel insecure."

Paul and I talked to Ellen a lot during the afternoon. I'd broken the ice the hard way, but we seemed to be able to speak about anything after that. She encouraged us to ask questions, so I asked if people who were blind from birth dream. "They dream in sounds and smells," Ellen said, "but if they ever had sight— even just a little—they dream as if they can see."

The clients at the Center knew lunch was coming way before we did.

"Franks and sauerkraut," Marty shouted.

"Broccoli," someone said.

"Skip that for me and give me two of something else," Belle added.

This time Joe showed us how to help as a man wheeled in a cart and dished food up onto plastic plates. "The food is arranged on the plates like a clock," Joe explained to us. "Stan, you got your meat at five o'clock," Joe said to a client, "sauerkraut at seven o'clock and broccoli at twelve. You want me to cut anything up?" When Stan was seated at the far end of the table Joe whispered to us, "They must eat by themselves. No feeding them. You never want people to feel helpless."

When Joe said that, something clicked. Everyone here was doing something he or she felt proud of. I thought about Ted, the pool captain, with nothing to do but boss people around and steal rolls in restaurants. And I got an idea. At the Center for the Blind, I could see clearly. But I didn't say anything about my idea yet.

The buses came and we helped the people onto them. Then we climbed back into Joe's station wagon. Paul sat in back with me again. I couldn't believe how fast the day had gone. On the way home we all talked at once. At the Center we'd seen all kinds of people helping each other. And most amazingly, for one whole day Grandma and Grandpa didn't comment on anyone's shoes, or even see the shoe stores we passed on the way back to Lemon Cove. That was the first day they didn't mention their old business.

"The blind leading the blind," Joe said. I thought of Doc Levinson, and the old saying made new sense to me.

Then something else dawned on me, something equally important. It suddenly seemed to me that the people at Lemon Cove were the ones who were blind. But my idea might change things. Today had been the best day of the vacation so far. If my plan worked, tomorrow would be even better!

# 8
# GETTING IT ALL TOGETHER

---

Dear Mom and Dad,

There's so much to tell you. I learned so much about some blind people today. It made me "see" things clearly.

Love,
Stacy (& Marc)

P.S. How do you know if you're in love?
P.P.S. Marc says he thinks he's forgotten how to swim. He'll explain when he sees you.

---

On day eight it rained, so we didn't get to the pool. At first we were disappointed, because we'd only have two more days in Florida and we had hardly been swimming at all. But we ended up having so much fun that swimming didn't seem as important as it had a week ago. Besides, last night's Chanukah gift was water colors with a note that said, "To splash around whenever you want."

When we celebrated the sixth night of Chanukah last night, the seven flickering candles looked extra nice. After the day at the Center for the Blind, I was glad I could see.

For dinner last night Grandma took my suggestion about home cooking—well, almost. The only dinner Grandma had cooked so far was the night we were all angry and silent. And who could eat? So last night, when she was looking at the newspaper, deciding which early bird dinner we should go to, I hinted about home cooking. She clipped this ad for me, and off we all went to

MAMA'S KOSHER KITCHEN
HOME COOKING
WE'RE THE BEST!
THURSDAY NIGHT SPECIAL DAIRY DINNER
REAL BLINTZES

To me Grandma's home cooking is the best, but I'd only hinted, and I figured Grandma might be too tired to cook after baking all those cookies at the Center. Tomorrow I'd tell Gandma how much I love *her* home cooking, then we'd eat all together, at home, laughing and talking.

"The owners of Mama's Kosher Kitchen retired and moved from Brooklyn," Grandpa explained when we got to the restaurant. "But after they were in Florida a while, they decided to open this restaurant. It tastes like home—Brooklyn cooking."

"I heard at the pool that the food is very good at this place," Grandma said. "I think I heard it from Ted."

98

I liked the owner, Mr. Frisher. He was kind of pear-shaped and he smiled a lot. The place was crowded—there was even a line of people waiting to be seated. Mr. Frisher made us feel as if we were in his home. He didn't just say, "You'll have to wait for a table," he said, "Come in. You're welcome. In a minute we'll have a table cleaned off just for you. Mrs. Frisher supervises all the cooking herself," he added.

Ted was at one of the tables. I don't know if Grandma and Grandpa noticed, but I nudged Marc so he'd see Ted pushing away his half-eaten noodle pudding and demanding that he not be charged. The owner quieted him, didn't charge him, and even gave him a fresh portion to take home. I remembered Joe saying Ted used to be a waiter. He seemed to know all the tricks for getting a free meal.

Now this Friday morning of day eight, I asked Grandma to make her creamy oatmeal. She made it without a single lump. Just like it used to do in Brooklyn, the steam made my bangs curl. As we ate, we talked about yesterday.

"You know," Grandma said, as she watched a pat of butter melt into the cereal, "Grandpa and I plan to go with Reggie and Joe a couple of days a week when they work at the Center for the Blind. Last night we discussed it during the Johnny Carson show."

"I think that's super," I said, and I kissed her cheek. Grandma was talking about tomorrows, and for the first time since we were here I didn't feel like I wanted *everything* as it used to be—just some things.

"Eat while it's hot," Grandma said, pointing to the cereal. And I smiled and took a mouthful.

"Can I go back to the Center with you next time I visit?" I asked.

"Me, too?" Marc said between mouthfuls.

"Of course," Grandpa answered, rubbing his full stomach and adding his old Brooklyn line to tease Grandma: "Now. What's for breakfast?"

"Grandpa," Marc answered as he always used to, "that *was* breakfast."

After breakfast Reggie, alias "Painter Lady," phoned to invite us all to her art room. We got ready and walked two doors down the catwalk. The Feldmans were happy to see us. They were dressed in jeans and old work shirts with paint spots. Their apartment was like Grandma's and Grandpa's, but the bedroom was on the right instead of the left, and they had wild paintings on the walls and lots of plants and C.B. equipment and photography stuff and easels and paints. One wall was filled with photographs of their grandchildren at dance recitals and bar mitzvahs and baseball games.

I was surprised—and really glad—when the doorbell rang and it was Lisa and Paul *and* their grandparents. I didn't know Reggie had phoned them, too. Paul introduced us. His grandparents were both wearing white slacks and flowered print tops. His grandfather's hair was curled in a gray Afro, and he wore his shirt unbuttoned and his chest hair stuck out. He also wore a heavy gold chain. I wondered why Lisa and Paul's grandparents just stayed in the doorway.

"Good to see you again," Paul and Lisa's grandfather said to the grown-ups. "Don't you just love

Lemon Cove?" their grandmother asked. "I feel like a kid again."

Before anyone had a chance to answer, they were on their way. "Have fun," they called. "We'll see you after the bridge game. We'd really love to stay, but our calendar is so filled. We're booked for a month in advance." It was obvious that Paul was disappointed to see them go.

Reggie said we could be creative until noon, when we'd have lunch and settle the "should-we-apologize-for-our-rebellious-act-or-not" issue.

"All suggestions will be welcome," Grandpa added. Then he stared at the blank white canvas in front of him. "I never could draw a straight line," he said.

"Crooked lines are much nicer, anyway," I said. "They're more interesting." Grandpa pinched my cheek and reached for a brush.

Reggie showed us how to mix oil paints and yet keep the colors from getting muddy by not using more than three colors at a time. Joe, Marc, and Lisa were taking photographs of all of us together. Lisa loved trying out words to make us smile at the camera.

"Smile and say dive." She laughed as we all went along with her suggestion. "Now say splash."

Joe called Paul to join him and take photographs. "I'd rather paint," Paul said. Then he set up his easel next to me. I couldn't believe it.

The air filled with a combination of oil paint smells and Old Spice after-shave lotion. My sensitive nose told me that. Today Paul, like Marc, was wearing after-shave lotion. Paul might even shave, though—

not real hairs yet, but fuzz. I could understand that. After all, I've worn a training bra for a year.

We all had so much fun together. We talked about so many things, like what it was like in the 1920s when our grandparents and the Feldmans grew up—real history. They didn't have electronic games; a lot of houses didn't even have electric lights. And Grandpa had to go to the corner candy store to use a phone. Then we talked about now: what it's like at a school dance, and my first baby-sitting job—how the little girl colored her teeth red with crayon while I went to the refrigerator to get her juice.

We enjoyed each other's stories. What I liked best was when Grandpa told us a mischievous thing he'd done as a kid. "Used to steal potatoes. Roasted them in an old can till they were charred and delicious. No potato ever tasted as good since," he said. "Right, Joe?"

"Right," Joe said, focusing his camera. "Remember sneaking into the movies?" Grandpa smiled ear to ear.

"Many of the retired people at Lemon Cove, including your Grandpa," Grandma explained, "have worked since they were eight or nine years old, believe it or not."

"Sold newspapers at eight, lied about my age and drove a truck at fourteen," Grandpa said.

"And these people became businesspeople and teachers, doctors and firefighters even," Reggie added.

"And bums," Grandpa joked, "some became bums, too. Now they just act like big shots," he went on. The muscles in his arms tightened. "Maybe because they feel useless. That mandatory retirement law should be illegal! Some people don't know how *not* to work." As Grandpa spoke, sounding a little like Herb, the Gray Panther, he painted shapes like people in crowds.

I looked at him. I'm not crazy about lectures, but I had the feeling he was talking about himself, and that made me listen. Why did everything have to stop just because you're sixty-five? It didn't for Joe, or Herb, or even the owners of Mama's Kosher Kitchen.

"Feeling hungry reminds some of these people of scary things," said Joe. "Lots of them went hungry when they were kids, and again later on during the Depression.

"Maybe food and love mean the same to them," Paul said.

"Grandma and Grandpa sure love us a lot," Lisa joked and snapped a photo of Marc photographing Paul and me.

I had started painting memories, some of the Center for the Blind, and some of Lemon Cove. I love to paint, except in art class, where if you don't paint trees green the kids think you're weird. My thoughts were interrupted as Paul held out his hand.

"Stacy, you want a Tic Tac?" he asked, but he didn't look at me, and, funny, his *not* looking at me made me feel like he was. I couldn't explain it, even to myself.

"Sure." I reached out for the small white candy.

"Tic Tacs, the answer to chewing gum for kids with braces," Paul joked.

"And I guess for older people with false teeth," Grandpa said and laughed. He reached out for a couple of pieces. "See, old and young have a lot in common."

I sucked on the Tic Tac and looked at my painting. I always get filled with thoughts when I paint. All my blind people looked alike. And all the old people I'd painted looked alike, too. My ideas were getting clearer in my mind, but not on the canvas. A lot of blind people don't need centers, I was thinking. They're too busy being college teachers or lawyers or singers or carpenters. I read that somewhere—I should have clipped the article. I added working blind people around the top edge of my canvas, but I didn't paint them very well. Sometimes my brush made a big blob of paint, but I knew what it was supposed to be. I painted the man who tuned our piano at home. He was blind, but he even poured his own coffee from a thermos without spilling a drop.

Then I thought about the old people I'd painted. Some were chained to their chained-down chairs. On the bottom of my canvas I showed them doing all sorts of things. Mixed in with my stick figures of retired people, I painted in young people, too, and older people at work or school. Suddenly I wondered if Grandma and Grandpa hadn't thought they *had* to retire to Florida, like Cinderella marrying the prince, everyone supposed to live happily ever after. But so many people seem so angry.

For a while it was very quiet, because we were all concentrating. I didn't even realize Reggie had left the room till I smelled peanut butter and coffee.

"I like your painting," Paul said as he walked to the table.

"Picasso, move over," Grandpa teased as he sat next to me.

Grandma even let us kids have a cup of coffee each, though she kept saying to put more milk in it. Reggie made sandwiches. We sipped the coffee and ate lunch and got down to business.

"I hate to spoil a beautiful day, but we're going to have to face the people at the pool," Grandpa said. "No more stalling. We have to decide on a plan right away."

I couldn't stop staring at a sandwich crumb stuck to Grandpa's lower lip. If he hadn't licked it off, I don't think I would have heard another word.

"Just apologize," Grandpa suggested.

"I can't apologize for something I'm not sorry about," I said. "It would be like telling a lie." The peanut butter felt stuck in my throat, and I took a sip of coffee.

"We'd better discuss that further," Grandpa said. "You mean you're not sorry for that rumpus and for upsetting elderly people and unraveling someone's knitting?"

"I'm a little sorry," I said, giving in. "But I'm more sorry I had to do it." That was about the best I could do.

"We didn't hurt anyone or anything," Marc added.

"Maybe you could bend the truth?" Grandma said. "Like say 'I'm sorry for what happened down here' and not say the rest, but mean you're sorry to see all these people sitting around."

"Grandma, that wouldn't be honest," Marc said, as

if he'd never told a lie in his life. He can look so innocent sometimes.

"I've got an idea," Paul said. "We could make a time capsule of condominium life in Florida and bury it for future generations. And in it we could put a tiny note that said 'We're sorry.' I'm studying archaeology in Social Studies," he added and sipped some coffee.

"They won't let you bury it," Lisa said, accidentally kicking the table leg. We all steadied our shaking cups. "You're not allowed to walk on the grass, much less dig a hole in it."

I laughed, picturing what future generations would think a hundred years from now if they discovered a time capsule from Lemon Cove. It would contain at least three bathing caps—one flowered—a plastic nose guard, hair scooped from the pool, a DON'T WALK ON THE GRASS sign, and one hundred bottles and tubes of suntan lotion.

"That's funny, Paul." I couldn't help laughing again, so I explained what I thought would be in the time capsule. "But we can't do that. It wouldn't be fair to future archaeologists. It would drive them crazy. They'd think the list of rules was some form of dictatorship. Listen, we've only got two days left. I got this idea yesterday. Want to hear it? It's not going to be easy, but I think it might work. We wouldn't actually have to apologize in words."

"Let's hear it, Stace," Grandpa said.

"I thought of it yesterday at the Center for the Blind," I said. Everyone was quiet, waiting to hear my idea. Reggie and Grandma didn't even start clearing the table. They waited and listened.

"Yesterday, at the Center, when Joe said we don't feed the blind people because they must never feel useless, I thought about the people at the pool. Take Ted, for instance. He's kind of the leader here," I said, "but I've been watching him. I think besides feeling useless, he has a money problem. At the restaurant I saw him stuffing leftover rolls into a plastic bag. And again last night after eating half his meal, he complained it was spoiled so he wouldn't have to pay."

"He probably doesn't have as much money to live on as he planned—because of inflation," Joe said.

"Everything costs so much more each year, but his Social Security only goes up a little," Reggie added.

"Put the milk away before it spoils," Grandma said to Reggie as if she was one of us kids. Reggie got up.

"Don't waste steps and go in with an empty hand," Grandpa said and handed Reggie his dish.

"If Ted was busy working," I said, stirring my cold coffee, "he wouldn't have to make up rules to feel important."

"He'd be a good lion tamer," Marc suggested, and Lisa giggled.

"It's hard for older people to get jobs," Grandma reminded me.

"I know," I said, "that's why I was so excited when I found these." I reached into my shorts pocket. "Last night when I couldn't sleep I clipped stuff from the newspaper, and I found these want ads." I smoothed them out on the table so everyone could see. I read one out loud.

WANTED—AIRPORT SECURITY GUARD—
UNIFORM PROVIDED.
FLEXIBLE HOURS—PART TIME. GOOD SALARY.
APPLICANT MUST BE ABLE TO GIVE DIRECTIONS
AND ENFORCE PARKING REGULATIONS.

"That's Ted," Paul said. "It's absolutely a description of Ted!"

"You know," Joe said, resting his chin on his hand, "I bet he would love to do that."

"What about the other people who are so angry at all of you for your rebellion?" Grandpa reminded us. "That sounds like a great idea for Ted, but you can't expect all those people to welcome you at the pool, you know. And you can't find jobs for them all. Not everyone wants to work. And . . . they're still going to insist that Marc wear a bathing cap."

Joe got a twinkle in his eye, and I knew he was up to something.

Paul moved closer to me and looked right into my eyes when I spoke. I almost couldn't get the words out. I cleared my throat and hoped I wasn't blushing as I went on with the results of my people watching.

"Here's how we could help the others feel useful," I went on. I pulled out that old ad for an acupuncture open house and read it.

ACUPUNCTURE OPEN HOUSE
SUNDAY 10–4

"Acupuncture? You're going to stick pins in them?" Grandma said.

"It's the open house part that I mean," I laughed. "We could have an open house at the pool. We could all get to know each other and learn things from each other like we're doing here today, and like we did yesterday at the Center. We could show we want to be friends, not enemies. Maybe we could even get permission to do a diving and swimming demonstration, or a race. We're all on swim teams at home."

I turned to Paul. "Maybe your grandparents could teach us to play bridge. They're interested in that. And that man with the garden. I could sure learn from him."

"We've got nothing to lose," Reggie said. "I'd love a day like that."

"No coffee and cake at the pool," Lisa added. "It's a rule."

"We could let everyone know tonight that there's an open house at the pool tomorrow, a surprise for everyone," Grandpa said. "But"—and he looked at Marc—"what about the bathing cap situation?" Grandma reached over and hugged Marc protectively.

Joe surprised us. "Yes," he said, eyes twinkling again. "Bring bathing caps. Bring all the bathing caps you can carry and plastic wrap and plastic bags, too. I've got some other equipment to gather," he said. "I saw this old blackboard at the flea market at the Sunrise Drive-In theater. I've got an idea for replacing the rules sign. The blackboard was bargain priced. It'll be my donation to a worthy cause. We'll meet at ten forty-five tomorrow at the pool—fully equipped."

Just before sundown Grandma opened the freezer and took out frozen chicken and matzo-ball soup. We had instant Grandma-cooked dinner, like I'd asked for. But we didn't eat home. We went to the Jewish Center for a Friday night community dinner and Sabbath service. It was special tonight, because it was also the seventh night of Chanukah. All I'd asked for was a home cooked meal, together. But I hadn't said where. Still, being together at services was like we used to do in Brooklyn, so I didn't mind. In fact, I liked it. We're not very religious, but Grandma always made Friday nights special.

After services, families kissed and wished each other *Shabbat Shalom*, which means "Good Sabbath" in Hebrew. Eight candles flickered in the beautiful big menorah at the Jewish Center.

There were about a hundred people there and no one seemed cross all evening. Everyone brought food and helped clean up. There was a piano that wasn't locked —anyone could use it, even kids. People sang Yiddish songs. I hummed along, except when I knew a word or two. Grandma and Grandpa knew all the words, and they said they'd teach them to Marc and me.

Tonight's Chanukah presents had no wrapping and they melted in your mouth: chocolate chocolate-chip cookies. Grandma must have made them early this morning. I thought I'd smelled something good when I woke up.

At bedtime I felt worried about tomorrow. Would

we be laughed at, or worse, by the people at the pool? I looked at the plastic bags and wrap Joe wanted us to bring, but I couldn't figure out what he wanted to do with them.

Only two days left, and so much to do!

# 9
# THE TALENT
# OPEN HOUSE

I'll never forget day nine, our next to last day at Lemon Cove. Grandpa cooked his special cereal pancakes made from eggs and cornflakes. He pretended he was a great chef, like he used to do in Brooklyn. At 10:45 we all went down to the pool to help Joe and Reggie take down the rules sign and put up the blackboard.

It was a beautiful sunny day, with fresh-smelling air and really blue sky, a perfect day for swimming. And, of course, the pool was empty and inviting. But we didn't go in—yet. Marc and I put down the shopping bag of bathing caps, plastic wrap, and plastic bags. Joe still wouldn't tell us what he planned to do with them.

Joe was struggling with his tool box, and Reggie, Paul, and Lisa were helping him. Grandma and Grandpa admired the big blackboard Joe had bought at the flea market.

I read again part of the want ad that I planned to give to Ted.

WANTED—AIRPORT SECURITY GUARD
APPLICANT MUST BE ABLE TO GIVE DIRECTIONS.

Perfect, I thought, and put the ad in my pocket. But would he rip it up or read it?

Reggie handed me a carton full of bathing caps and I added the shopping bag full of bathing caps and stuff Marc and I had collected since yesterday. I couldn't believe it! One bathing cap looked like imitation hair. No matter how we begged, Joe wouldn't explain.

"You'll see," he said. A twinkle in his eyes told me he was enjoying our curiosity.

At eleven o'clock, as if a bell rang, people started arriving at the pool, headed for their usual places. The woman with the white ointment on her nose stared at us from her chair. Around his neck Ted hung his heavy wood block engraved with TED–POOL CAPTAIN. Then he started toward us. Mrs. Roth with the crooked toes arranged herself on a lounge chair and the man with the hairy chest and a cigar in his mouth stood near Joe, watching.

Lisa handed me chalk, and I wrote the message for the day on the blackboard. We'd planned it last night. People gathered around as I wrote

LET'S BE FRIENDS
TALENT OPEN HOUSE
FREE
SHARE YOUR SKILLS AND LEARN NEW ONES

Somehow a good plan felt better than an apology I didn't mean. Our compromise seemed good and I hoped it would be accepted.

More people came to the pool. One woman dumped her beach bag onto the table to find her

113

glasses so she could read what we'd written. Mrs. Roth asked to borrow the glasses. People at Lemon Cove borrow each other's glasses a lot.

Those other kids didn't even open their Monopoly set today. They handed it back to their grandparents and walked over to us. Almost everyone looked interested. The kids were probably surprised to read something that wasn't a rule. At first the adults seemed suspicious. Maybe they expected us to blow the place up or turn the sprinklers on them, like we might have wanted to do a few days ago. But after they read the message, some people just shrugged their shoulders.

"I don't understand," a man with a beard said in a booming voice.

"It doesn't sound bad. Let's wait and see," said a woman with every hair in place, as if she just came from a beauty parlor.

Then Ted said the dreaded magic words to Marc: "Are you going to wear a bathing cap today?" Ted looked at Marc, daring him.

Before Marc had a chance to answer, Joe pointed to the carton of bathing caps and kicked it. Ted scratched his head, not understanding. "I'll explain in a minute," Joe said, busily loosening the last screw holding up the big rules sign.

"Are you destroying that sign?" the woman with the ointment on her nose called to Joe.

"No, Mrs. Newman," Joe answered. "I'm just exercising my rights as the pool fix-it person," Joe said as he replaced the rules sign with the new blackboard, which Paul, Lisa, and I had handed him. Now my ad could be seen clearly.

"There are a few things that really need fixin'
around here," Joe added. "And the first event of the
day will be my special report to the people. It's been
two months since I volunteered to be the pool care-
taker. You've watched me fix things up around here,
but you haven't offered to help or acted on any of the
grievances I submitted to the grievance committee—
in writing, as required."

"Maybe they've been referred to the Central
Grievance Committee," Mrs. Newman answered. The
white ointment on her lips was shiny in the sunlight.
"Important decisions take time, you know," she added.

"All the committees do is set up more committees,"
Joe complained. "Anyway, to get back to my special
report: we all need to be careful with our money, and
I've saved you dollars and cents."

I wrote on the blackboard

## 1. JOE'S SPECIAL MONEY-SAVING REPORT

"I have good news for you and bad news," Joe said,
clearing his throat. "First, the good news. I have saved
the residents of this condominium $105.50 per month.
I've taken care of cleaning the pool filter and fixing
any lounge chairs that break. I've repaired the sprinklers and the pool ladder, and the folding umbrellas
now fold once again."

Ted started a round of applause. We all joined in.

"Now for the bad news," Joe said. He put his arm
around Reggie and I waited to hear the news, too,
because he hadn't mentioned anything about bad news
last night.

Joe cleared his voice once again and announced, "Reggie and I may be putting our apartment up for sale. We are thinking of moving into a house where our own grandchildren can have fun and will want to visit. We want to enjoy watching them without shushing and saying no all the time."

"Don't move away, Joe," I found myself calling. I was glad Grandma and Grandpa had friends close by to help them get used to their new life in Florida— friends like Reggie and Joe, who still loved kids.

"Please don't move," Paul shouted. Some others around the pool joined in pleading for Joe and Reggie to stay. But not everyone.

"We're wrong to want peace and quiet?" the man with the towel on his head asked. "We did for our kids when we were younger. Now it's time to think of ourselves. We paid our dues already."

"Why didn't you object to the rules at the grievance meetings?" the ointment woman—Mrs. Newman— asked.

"We always have objected," Reggie said, "but no one here listens."

"I'll still come back and help you people with the pool and all," Joe said, "because I know you need the help and because I enjoy fixing things. We won't move far away, we'll just move to freedom. And about peace and quiet, I'll have years of quiet when I die. Peace I have here and now when I help another person." Joe had everyone's attention.

"You'd still help us? Even if you moved away?" asked Mrs. Newman, smearing still more ointment on her nose and lips.

"But," Ted said, "we have to have rules. If we'd had stronger rules, maybe there wouldn't have been rec room damage."

"What damage?" I asked. We hadn't damaged anything.

"The pool table is scratched," Ted answered.

"I did that," an older man with a flowered bathing suit admitted shyly. The cigar he smoked had an ash about an inch long and his wife cupped her hands to catch the ash if it fell.

"Thank you, Burt, for being honest," Joe said. "Accidents will happen."

"Well, maybe we wouldn't have had to hire a security guard at vacation time when the children are here," Ted went on. "Then maybe I wouldn't have to think about moving to a less expensive place." He muttered the last sentence almost under his breath. He seemed embarrassed. But I heard what he said, and so did Paul and some of the others. "Some Golden Age," Ted said. "You can't even afford a penny to spare for bingo."

Then Joe wrote on the blackboard:

## 2. THE CHILDREN SPEAK

I found my heart pounding. I always felt like my bones were melting whenever I had to speak anywhere, even in front of my class at school. But I didn't want Joe to move away and, much to my surprise, I found I didn't want Ted to move away, either, now that I'd started to understand why he acted the way he did.

117

I cleared my throat and stood as tall as I could. First I took the ad out of my pocket, smoothed it out, and handed it to Ted. Paul flashed me the sign that means "you're doing okay."

"Please read this," I said. "It might help."

Then I spoke to everyone. When something is important, I guess you just find the right words to talk about it. "Maybe Joe and Reggie and Ted could all stay," I said. "You wouldn't have to change all the rules, just the ones that don't make sense. And maybe Joe and Reggie's grandchildren would love it here if there were interesting things for all of us to do. We could learn so much from all of you. And we could show you a couple of interesting things, too."

I peeked at Ted. He *was* reading the ad, and I felt there was hope until I saw him crumple it up. But at least he didn't throw it away. He just stuffed it into his pocket, muttering, "Like the other employers, when they see you're old they say the job is filled already." I was worried again that my idea might not work.

Paul took over just when I thought my knees would give out. I couldn't believe I had spoken out like that in front of people, even adults.

"We'd like to give a swimming and diving demonstration at two thirty tomorrow, if it's all right with you, and swimming lessons to anyone who is interested, tomorrow at three o'clock," Paul announced.

"Put it in writing," Mrs. Newman said. "We'll form a committee to decide."

"I'll chair that committee," Grandpa volunteered.

"Me, too," Grandma added.

"Trouble ahead," I said to Paul when Mrs. White-

Lips Newman signed up to be on the committee. So did the man with the cigar and his wife—and Ted.

Paul and Lisa went over to their grandparents and whispered to them. Then with a big smile, Lisa announced, "My grandmother and grandfather have volunteered to be on the diving and swimming demonstration committee, too. And today at noon, right here at this table, they'll give bridge lessons to the children. My brother Paul and I are going to be in their group."

Grandma started right in campaigning. "Lots of times I've heard some people complain how they never learned to swim," Grandma said, "but swimming you can learn at any age." She proudly pointed to us. "These are such good swimmers and such nice children. They could teach you. Wait, you'll see for yourself. And," she added, "to those who have admired the needlepoint I'm making, I'd like to give a demonstration in that corner over there"—she pointed —"at noon today. Children welcome."

Reggie was making a sign-up list on the blackboard under 3. ACTIVITIES. She added her own portrait-painting demonstration at 2:00—"model needed." The girl in the toothpaste striped bathing suit said, "How about me? I'm good at sitting still." And her grandmother laughed and hugged her.

Grandpa spoke to the man with the garden, who smiled shyly. "Mr. Cohen and I will talk to the children about plants," Grandpa announced, "at two thirty at Mr. Cohen's garden." Reggie wrote that on the blackboard, too.

Marc kept on staring at the big carton of bathing caps.

Grandpa spoke again. "There's not much we can do about *this* vacation. Tomorrow is our grandchildren's last day. I like peace and quiet as much as anyone else, but on Christmas and Easter vacations I like to hear children enjoying, and I like to enjoy with them. I figured out that for the same price we paid for a guard for Christmas vacation, we could pay for planned programs for Easter vacation that would be fun for all of us. Bingo and Ping-Pong tournaments with prizes. And we could all even put on a show together and get to know each other and each other's families. Maybe we could hire a college student on vacation to run things and supervise in the clubhouse so everyone can use it with only a couple of no's."

"Maybe we could do *Fiddler on the Roof,*" suggested the same woman who last week had said "Weren't you ever a child?" "I used to be a director in a summer camp," she added. "If whoever has the key would unlock the piano in the rec room, I'll play for the children. I even know rock and roll."

"Or maybe we could write our own show." The man with the cigar puffed as he spoke. "I've always wanted to try something like that."

Of course there were also a lot of people who just waved as if to say "Oh go away" or "Get lost." And one man went right over and turned up the volume of the pool radio to drown us out. Another woman turned off her hearing aid. She lay back on the lounge chair and went to sleep. A group of four people gave us dirty looks and left.

But I know that sometimes it's hard to get used to changes. Oh boy, do I know that. I still had to get used to all those new kids and teachers in junior high school. But now I was ready. If someone told me my sneakers are all wrong or something, I'd give a Ted look and vaporize the kid! Or a Joe joke and say, "You think my sneakers are weird, you should see my feet!"

And I know how sometimes you can't say things or apologize. That's why I even began to understand Ted. At least Ted had listened. He turned to Joe and said, "I hope we both can stay here and be friends. Which rule do you want changed the most?"

"Well, this bathing cap business," Joe said, "makes no sense at all. I'm the one who takes care of the pool. Hairs don't hurt the pool. That's why there are filters. That's what they're for, to catch hairs and bugs and stuff." Joe pointed to Marc, who was wearing his innocent face. "So if this boy's hair will ruin the pool— if *he* has to be made to wear a bathing cap against his will—then so do you, Mr. Razmussin." Joe turned to this bald man who had a long white beard. Joe reached into the carton filled with caps and handed Mr. Razmussin a flowered bathing cap. "If that doesn't fit, here's a plastic bag," he added.

A smile grew on Marc's face as he caught on to Joe's plan. Paul stood close to me, and our shoulders touched. I'm not sure if it was on purpose. I hoped it was.

"And Burt," Joe called to the heavyset man with the cigar, "you have more hair on your chest than this boy has on his head." Joe chuckled as he handed Burt a roll of clear plastic wrap. Paul, Marc, Lisa, and I

were headed for a good old giggling-snorting fit, when Joe turned to Ted and said, "Ted, if you don't want hair in the pool, you'd better shave your legs."

Then Joe dumped out the box of bathing caps. "Either everyone has to wear caps, plastic bags, or wrap wherever they have hair, or no one has to."

Lots of people were chuckling by now. But a couple in the corner on lounge chairs got up and said, "You're all crazy." They left muttering, "You can't get any peace of mind around here."

Ted said out loud, "All in favor of eliminating the bathing cap rule say aye."

Ted said, "Aye," and a lot of other people did, too. There were only a few grumbles.

"Anyone against?" Ted asked, and not a hand was raised, probably because anyone who was against eliminating the bathing cap rule, or making any other changes, had left.

Marc looked around in amazement. The flapping sound of a duck in the distant canal seemed like applause. Ted and Joe shook hands. It was noon, and the pool area suddenly was full of activity as we broke up into groups.

Marc, Lisa, Paul, and I took bridge lessons. "Your grandparents are really good players," I said to Paul when he leaned over to help me fix the cards in my hand. I could feel his breath on my neck. It distracted me.

"You kids sure learn fast," Paul's grandfather said when Paul and Lisa played.

"Too bad tomorrow is your last day here," their grandmother said. "Next time you visit we'll play cards with you." She reached out and hugged Paul on one side and Lisa on the other, and Lisa and Paul hugged back.

I already knew how to do needlepoint, from a club in school, but it was new for Marc. He let Grandma teach him and Lisa. From Mr. Cohen, Paul and I learned how marigolds crowd each other out if you don't leave enough space for each plant, and how a schifflera tree grows up to thirty feet high.

We couldn't resist Reggie's 2:00 portrait class after Ted told us he'd be the next model. I think he enjoyed the attention. A lot of the other kids at the pool joined this group also. However, with about twenty kids, but only about twenty adults, I realized our open house was not a huge success. There are at least a thousand people living in Lemon Cove, of which two hundred and fifty use this pool—Grandpa and Grandma were explaining that in a restaurant we were in last week.

At three o'clock about thirty more people, the Central Grievance Committee, appeared at the pool. Mrs. Roth read an announcement out loud in her rough voice: "Everyone has a right to peace and quiet. All pool activities must be scheduled one day in advance, in writing. And there must be a quiet time from twelve P.M. to two P.M. for those who prefer it."

Actually, that made sense to all of us.

"We were so excited about our open house we figured everyone would like it," I said to Grandpa and Joe.

"We can't make up people's minds for them," Joe added.

Paul took the bridge score pad and started to write.

## TOMORROW'S SCHEDULE

12–2 Quiet time, but because it's so hot everyone can go swimming, even kids
2–3 Sign up for activities: needlepoint, bridge, or gardening
3–3:30 Swimming and diving demonstration
3:30–4:00 Swimming lessons

Marc, Lisa, and I leaned over his shoulders to read the schedule. We all agreed it sounded fair, even though "fair" didn't always seem to matter in Lemon Cove, at least not so far this vacation.

Paul handed the written request to Mrs. Roth, who said, "Until the committee votes, this open house is closed." The Grievance Committee would bring its decision about tomorrow's activities up to my grandparents' apartment this evening, since the "should-there-be-a-swimming-diving-demonstration" committee would be meeting there at eight o'clock tonight.

"Rome wasn't built in a day," Grandma said—whatever that means.

One thing was settled, though, before we all went upstairs. Joe and Reggie agreed to stay on at Lemon Cove if the blackboard stayed up, so the blackboard was left in place of the rules sign.

"That way," Joe said, "if you need a rule you could write it on the blackboard, next to the word PLEASE, and you could erase the rule if it's not needed. And if you don't need a rule, you could write a nice message or a funny joke or the activity of the day."

"That's a great idea," I said.

Grandma cooked almond chicken for dinner, using the recipe I'd clipped and given her. It smelled wonderful as it cooked, especially the onions that were in it. It was a new smell, since Grandma had never made this recipe before, but there was something familiar about it, too: the combination of chicken, and Grandma and Grandpa and Marc and I, just us, together.

Before dinner we all helped Grandma make real potato pancakes, homemade. You're supposed to eat them on Chanukah to celebrate the oil lamp burning in the ancient temple for eight days on one day's oil supply. It's because the potato pancakes are cooked in oil that makes them special for Chanukah. Grandpa explained that to me a long time ago in Brooklyn.

Tonight, on the last night of Chanukah, we lit the candles, all eight of them plus the shammes lighting candle. We stood close together and watched them twinkle. They looked so pretty and smelled so good, and I knew that even after they were gone they'd still glow in my memory.

We all thought the chicken was delicious—except Marc, who picked out the nuts and onions but ate the meat. We agreed we had all enjoyed the open house and hoped we could have the diving demonstration tomorrow.

Grandpa said he was so proud of us. Grandma was, too. Our last Chanukah gift was an envelope. It was sealed and on it was written

TO STACY AND MARC
WITH LOVE FROM GRANDMA AND GRANDPA
DO NOT OPEN UNTIL YOU ARE ON THE AIRPLANE.

We hugged and kissed thank you. When we used to leave my grandparents' house in Brooklyn they used to give us a surprise note to read in the car. Marc tried to grab the envelope and hold it to the light, but I got it back and put it in my jeans pocket.

This had been a really exciting day, but the results of the night's meetings would tell if it had been a success or a failure. I couldn't wait to find out!

# 10
# THE VOTE

The Diving and Swimming Demonstration Committee met as scheduled in Grandma and Grandpa's living room at eight o'clock. People in Fort Lauderdale wear very colorful clothes, and the people on this committee reminded me of the peacocks at Turtle Back Zoo in New Jersey.

I was glad Grandma and Grandpa said they'd be the committee chairpersons.

"This is the first time we've gotten involved in condominium politics," Grandpa had said to me earlier.

"I went to one meeting," Grandma had said. "For a half hour people complained that the coffee was bitter. Who needs it? A waste of time." Then she'd patted me on the head. "This I'm doing for you and Marc."

Reggie and Joe had gone to hear the discussions at the Central Grievance Committee, since Joe was Pool Fix-it Person and they were discussing pool matters. Anyway, it would have been a fixed vote if besides Marc and my grandparents and Lisa and Paul's grandparents—the Coopers—we'd added Reggie and Joe. It wouldn't have been fair. So we had to win some votes from Ted or Mrs. Newman, alias White Lips, or Burt, the man with the cigar, or his wife.

The committee discussed whether or not we could dive, should dive, and would dive . . . in that order. It was really like politics on TV, smoke-filled room and all, thanks to Burt and his cigar. The Coopers had brought a big envelope. They opened it and pulled out a batch of letters and clippings about Paul's and Lisa's wins on the Morristown swim team. They laid the clippings out on the glass and chrome coffee table. Paul's times were impressive: thirty seconds in the backstroke and thirty-two in the butterfly.

"And Paul's going to be a doctor," his grandmother added as if that would take care of everything. Paul turned beet red.

A second later my cheeks were a matching color after Grandma whispered to me and nodded toward Paul, "He's cute, isn't he? You like the thirteen-year-old doctor, don't you?" My grandma has this whisper you can hear across the room. I know Grandpa heard it because he winked at me. At first I hoped Paul didn't hear. And then I hoped he did.

Grandma put out a dish of raisins and nuts. "To sweeten the disposition and aid the digestion," she joked. "First we'll take a vote just to see where we are, and then we'll discuss some more and vote again."

I could have told them the vote count in advance. It would be four in favor and four against the swimming and diving demonstration. And of course that's what it was.

"That's that," Mrs. Newman said. "If you check with Robert's Rules you'll see you don't discuss after you vote." She pushed her glasses back on her pale

129

nose and took out her knitting from the shopping bag marked Atlantic Federal Bank.

"Who's Robert Rules?" Grandma asked, passing around the raisins and nuts.

"Rules, shmules," Grandpa said. "We're the chair-persons. There's a job to be done. Let's do it."

Grandma must have wanted to soothe Mrs. Newman, because she said, "That's a beautiful sweater you're knitting."

"It's for my granddaughter," Mrs. Newman said. "I make all her sweaters. She wears them at Boston University and is on the honor roll." It sounded to me like Mrs. Newman's sweaters got you on the honor roll. I pictured Mrs. Newman back in the rec room the other day, with the runaway chair and trail of unraveling yarn. Grandma had picked the wrong subject. Marc and Lisa even stopped playing rummy and listened.

"This sweater would have been done already if it wasn't for you-know-who." Mrs. Newman glared at Marc and Lisa.

Grandma is quick, though. She changed the subject. "Marc and Lisa," she said, "go get the seltzer, milk, and chocolate syrup out. There's nothing like a nice egg cream on a hot night. Maybe you two could make them for all of us," she added.

"I'll vote yes on having a cold drink," Ted said, emphasizing the drink part as if that might be the only thing he would vote yes about.

I kept quiet. Paul was sitting next to me on the couch and Burt, the man with the cigar, and his wife, took up a lot of room on the other side of me. Paul and I were kind of squished together. I was glad we were close, but I was afraid to move. Maybe Paul was quiet for the same reason.

Lisa and Marc, on the other hand, were not quiet. The kitchen is next to the living room, and I could hear Lisa's voice clearly. "Not so much seltzer. It's fizzing over. I told you so," she said.

"Grandma, where's the sponge?" Marc called.

"In the sink," Grandma called back.

Ted got up and went to help Marc. "Mopped up many an egg cream in my day," Ted said proudly.

I couldn't stop staring at Burt. Not because of his bright red shirt and white pants, but because I never saw a cigar with such a long ash. His wife cupped her hands under the cigar. "Be careful of the yellow couch," she said. "And don't burn a hole in your new shirt." After Grandma handed Burt an ashtray, his wife relaxed and leaned back.

I wondered when they'd get back to discussing the demonstration. I was beginning to understand why Robert's Rules of Order were used in meetings. I'd learned about them in Social Studies. But Grandma seemed in no hurry. "Where did you get that beautiful shirt?" she asked Burt as she sat down in her chair. I figured she must know what she's doing. They did stuff like complimenting in politics on TV.

"You like it?" Burt asked, flicking his cigar in the ashtray. "I bought this shirt and pants today. It was something to do."

Ted came in carrying the tray of drinks. "You

bought both the same day?" he said. "You could have taken two days to do that."

Grandma cut right in. "But tomorrow you could be busy enjoying a swimming and diving demonstration. It'll be a good change of pace. It will feel good."

"She's selling this idea like she used to sell shoes," I whispered to Paul. He has the nicest smile.

"Now let's vote," Grandpa said. Ted served the drinks and Lisa and Marc looked like angels as they gave out napkins. Lisa's grandmother pinched her cheek.

But Ted changed the subject back to shopping and the vote was delayed again. "Where'd you buy the shirt and pants?" he asked Burt, and I noticed Ted put his hand over a little hole in his own green shirt.

"The store over on University, the one with the snippy young owner," Burt answered.

"The store where the owner's own children took the sign BEWARE OF DOG out of the window and put in a sign that said BEWARE OF OWNER?" Paul's grandfather laughed.

"That's the place," Burt said.

"There's no respect these days," Ted mumbled. Maybe he was sorry to be out of drinks to serve. I wondered if he'd thrown out the job ad I'd given him. But he didn't mention it, and I wasn't about to ask.

"Don't spill your drink, Burt," his wife said. "Drink it quickly. There's yellow carpeting." Burt drank down the egg cream in a single gulp. He always seemed to do what his wife said. Marc gulped his drink down, too, but he usually does that. I like to sip mine. Anyway, I was afraid I'd burp. Egg creams make you do that and Paul was right next to me.

Grandma asked me and Marc if she could show our swim team clippings to win some votes. I was glad she asked.

"Okay," I said, "but not my letters."

She pulled the clippings out of her pants pocket. She was prepared, all right. Paul seemed interested in reading them, too. So did everyone else in the room except Mrs. Newman and Ted.

"Now let's vote again," Grandma said.

Only then Burt let out this most enormous burp. It sounded like the word itself. "Your shoes too tight?" Grandpa joked. He always says that when someone burps. I don't know what it means.

Grandma and Grandpa voted yes. And of course so did the Coopers. I wasn't surprised that Ted and Mrs. Newman voted no. That left Burt and his wife.

"You vote first," he said to her.

She didn't hesitate a minute. "I vote NO," she said.

Burt took his time. But he usually did whatever his wife said, so he'd probably vote the same, too. No is what I figured he'd say, and I'd be disappointed, after they'd listened to Grandma and read the clippings. I thought we'd had a good chance they'd vote in our favor. Burt made us wait for his answer just the way he lets the cigar ash get really long.

Wouldn't you know it—just then Marc, inspired by Burt's burp, started in. Marc is known in Plainfield Elementary School for his ability to burp the first four notes of Beethoven's Fifth. He learned it from the rock version of the song. I couldn't believe he'd do it here, but that's what he did. He burped "Wah wah wah WAH!"

"Disgusting," White Lips Newman said, and she almost dropped a stitch.

But Burt laughed. "I've met my match," he said. Then he flicked the ash on his cigar, looked straight at his wife, and voted, "Yes!"

I don't know if it was the burp that did it, but Marc is convinced it was. Burt even signed up for a three thirty swimming lesson.

There was a knock on the door. Grandpa opened it and Mr. Razmussin, the man Joe had given a beard bathing cap to, said, "I'm representing the Grievance Committee. Here is our report: After much arguing and debate the committee has approved tomorrow's activity schedule with a couple of changes." He stopped talking and waited. Everyone here seems to take their time when they have something important to do or say, I noticed.

"Go on," Grandpa said.

"There should be a longer quiet time, and a half-hour adults-only swim has been added," Mr. Razmussin said. "This is our final decision. Do you agree?" He kind of twisted his beard and looked at each of us.

"Sit down," Grandpa offered him a chair. "Take a load off your feet."

"I have to get back with the answer. They're waiting in the rec room on pins and needles," he added.

"Must be an acupuncture open house and Grievance Committee meeting," Paul whispered to me. It was good to be in on a joke with Paul.

"Everyone in favor of accepting the new schedule say aye." Grandpa sounded funny talking like Robert's Rules.

"Aye," we all said together. Well, not all.

"Naaaay," Mrs. Newman said, sounding like Black Beauty. "And I hope it rains tomorrow."

Would this meeting ever end? Did White Lips know how to say yes? Maybe she was always kind of nasty, even when she was a kid. There's this girl in my class who always votes no, no matter what.

"I don't know what all this fuss is about," Mrs. Newman went on talking. "All these changes. So much time discussing activities when we should be meeting about important things like removing the bush near the elevator. We don't want bushes around here. Someone could be lurking behind them at night."

She was really serious. She kind of shuddered when she spoke and her whole face got pale enough to match her nose and lips. I'd noticed that the women clutch their pocketbooks when they walk down the street, but I never thought maybe a lot of older people feel scared. Were they afraid of kids? Of us, their friends' grandchildren?

"That's a good matter for the Central Grievance Committee," Mr. Razmussin said to Mrs. Newman. "I'll bring it up at the next meeting."

"Getting back to the swimming and diving demonstration for tomorrow"—Grandpa got everyone's attention by clearing his throat—"the vote's five to three in favor."

"Tomorrow we'll show everyone at the pool that some kids can be trusted," I whispered to Paul and he nodded.

"Good," Mr. Razmussin said. "I'm looking forward to tomorrow."

I noticed his eyes got a sparkle in them like Joe's.

By 9:30 the meeting was over and the people left. I phoned Reggie and Joe to tell them the revised and approved schedule for tomorrow would include a swimming and diving demonstration. I read Joe the compromise schedule I'd written.

12–1 Quiet time, but because it's hot everyone can swim, even kids

1–1:30 Adults-only swim (that was for Mrs. Newman and a few others who were now the new minority)

1:30–2 Quiet time, but all can swim

2–3 Sign-up and activities—needlepoint, bridge, gardening, portrait drawing

3–3:30 Swimming and diving demonstration

3:30–4:00 Swimming lessons

"Joe?" I asked. "How many days did it take to build Rome?"

"A different amount for different people," he said, and I knew what he meant.

Before I went to bed I tried to guess what was inside the envelope, our Chanukah present. All I could tell was it was thicker than a check.

# 11
# THE OPEN HOUSE ...
# REVISITED

The morning of day ten, after a delicious breakfast of french toast (Grandma-made), Marc and I helped straighten up the apartment. Grandpa kind of gift-wrapped the garbage. First he emptied the pails into paper bags from the supermarket. Then he put the paper bags into plastic bags and folded down the top and stapled it.

"You want a ribbon to put on top?" Marc joked as he helped carry out the garbage.

"We have to wrap the garbage that way," Grandpa said. "It's a rule. But it makes sense. Who needs rats and bugs?"

Grandma likes to do everything herself, but I insisted on helping with the laundry. "The sheets are heavy," I said, "and I used a lot of towels. I wash my hair a lot."

"I noticed," Grandma said, putting some more towels into a fold-up shopping cart, the kind she used to wheel to the Waldbaum's supermarket in Brooklyn. "The last generation of teen-agers—the flower children —the flowers could have been planted in their hair, it was so dirty. And your generation, your hair is going to fall out you wash it so much. Listen to your grand-mother," she added. "You wash hair every few days and once a week you put an egg on it." She leaned over and sniffed my hair. "Not a lemon."

"An egg? That's gross," I said. But I liked this con-versation. We used to talk like this in Brooklyn.

"And bring me your laundry," Grandma ordered. "You should go home with clean clothes. Your moth-er's a working woman now. Selling real estate's not easy. I could at least help her with your laundry. I can do that long distance."

Grandma walked beside me as I pulled the shop-ping cart to the laundry room at the end of the cat-walk. It was sunny and hot, not even a gray cloud. Mrs. Newman hadn't put a hex on our diving dem-onstration.

In the laundry room there were a million rules taped to the walls—rules about lint removal and what detergents not to use. One machine was out of order and a sign said:

REPEAT REPAIR SERVICE WILL BE BACK
AGAIN NEXT WEEK TO FIX THE WASHER

"They come back again and again, just like their name," Grandma said, "not because it keeps breaking, but because they don't fix it right!" Grandma seemed to be cleaning invisible lint off the screen—in our dryer at home lint is never invisible. There was a newspaper on a chair near the washing machine, and I clipped an ad while Grandma put the stuff in the washer. She didn't want me to help like my mom does.

"I have to do this myself," Grandma said. So I let her.

This ad—for mirrors—gave me a funny image. The ad said

**MIRRORS**
**CUSTOM MADE**
**TO FIT ANY SIZE AND SHAPE**
**FREE IN-HOME ESTIMATES**
491–8559

I pictured mirrors in the shapes of the people at the pool. Pot bellies, or tall but slumped over with a pool captain necklace, or athletic. Maybe they make a mirror that holds knitting or has white lips. I clipped the ad to show to Marc.

When we got back to the apartment Grandpa was on the phone with Doc Levinson from the Center for the Blind. "Next Wednesday?" Grandpa said. He put his hand over the mouthpiece. "Can we work at the Center next Wednesday?" he asked Grandma.

"Of course we can," Grandma said. "If they need us we'll be there, tell him." And they both sounded happy. It made me happy, too, because although I kind of missed my parents, I was starting to feel bad about leaving Grandma and Grandpa. Or maybe I was feeling nervous because of the swimming and diving demonstration. I wanted to do well, after all.

We met Reggie and Joe and Paul and Lisa and their grandparents at the pool at noon. Reggie wrote the schedule for the day on the blackboard.

The pool area was a little more crowded than yesterday. During the adult swim six adults even swam. Today no one left until quiet time was over, and even then only about five people did. There'd been about sixty people, twenty kids and at least forty adults. I think some people walked over from one of the other pools. Maybe they'll start their own open house there.

Today lots more people signed up for activities. Even better, four more activity groups started: one in making shell earrings, one in learning Yiddish, one in learning Italian, and one in disco dancing. A lot of people just watched, but that was still better than yesterday. And I noticed that some of yesterday's watchers were doing stuff today.

"Come on, Mrs. Newman, let's boogie," I heard Mr. Razmussin say.

But at 3:00, when it came time for the diving and swimming demonstration, Mrs. Newman wiped off her white ointment and started to leave.

"Maybe you could just watch a little bit," I asked. "We don't want to chase you."

"You could sit in the back so you won't get splashed," Paul added.

"Why, thank you," Mrs. Newman said. "Maybe I'll watch from my terrace." She walked away.

Joe announced that the demonstration would begin. With cheers from the adults and other children, Lisa, Marc, Paul, and I gave the best swimming and diving demonstration ever—in this pool, anyway, which was easy because it was probably the only one. We had races and did special strokes, and none of us wore bathing caps. I did the crawl and the breaststroke and two perfect dives off the edge of the pool—the very deep end, of course. I didn't do backdives, because with no diving board it would have been dangerous. Paul demonstrated the backstroke, and Lisa and Marc did the butterfly.

The race was the best part of the afternoon.

"On your marks. Get set. Go!" Joe enjoyed giving that kind of order.

First I was overready and started diving before Joe said "Go." I kind of fell into the pool—a false start. When I came up I heard some people laugh, but not Paul. "That happens to me, too," he said. "C'mon. That was just practice." He reached down and helped me out of the pool.

"On your marks. Get set. Go!" Joe said once more.

This time I dove in at the right moment and it felt really good. I was breathing right, stroking hard and solid. The crawl is my best stroke. I scooped the water like ice cream, like my coach said: "Vanilla and chocolate, vanilla and chocolate," I told myself. When my head was above water I could hear the cheers. What a great sound! I didn't know who won at first, because when I reached the other end of the pool and looked up, I saw Paul.

Paul and I tied in that freestyle. Twenty seconds each. Terrific time, but of course it wasn't an Olympic-size pool. I think everyone applauded.

"Not bad," Paul said to me.

"Great time," I said. When we got out of the pool and Paul squeezed my hand, my heart sounded much louder than the applause.

Grandma hugged me. "A wonderful demonstration. Wonderful!" She said it very loudly.

"Like a couple of fish," Grandpa said. "Mark Spitz, move over."

Joe and Reggie shook my hand.

Mrs. Newman came back to the pool at 3:30 and watched the swimming lesson while she put more ointment on her nose and lips. Maybe she felt she couldn't be at the pool for the diving demonstration. It might be considered giving in.

During the lesson some people got out of their lounge chairs and sat at the edge of the pool, dangling their feet. We even gave a swimming lesson to Mrs. Roth, the woman with the crooked toes. At least we got her to float on her back. And of course Burt had his swim lesson. He even floated with a cigar in his mouth. Then suddenly, at 3:30, without a word, Ted very quietly walked away.

Day ten went by so fast. Before we knew it the sun was disappearing and people began talking about dinner plans for the first time all day. We heard some people saying as they left the pool, "A nice day. A very nice day." They didn't say it to us, just sort of to the sky. But we knew what they meant. And Mrs. Newman rubbed the white ointment off her nose and grumbled, "Not such a bad day, after all."

We were sorry now that this was our last day. Our plane was leaving at 9:00 P.M. It turned out that Paul and Lisa's grandparents had been able to switch tickets with someone else so we'd all be together on the same night flight back to New Jersey.

Today had been very exciting, but tonight still had some surprises in store.

# 12
# A TIME TO FLY

The evening of day ten we had pot roast for dinner. "Brisket," Grandma called it. "Not as lean as from the butcher on Avenue M in Brooklyn," she said, "but a nice taste of its own." We even had chocolate-pudding pie for dessert.

After dinner Grandma and Grandpa walked from room to room checking for things Marc or I had forgotten to pack. Grandpa found one sock under the couch and Grandma found a bottle of creme rinse inside the shower. I looked around the apartment, too, so I could remember it better. Marc followed me.

Grandpa and Joe insisted on carrying our suitcases down to the car without any help. Then my grandparents, the Feldmans, Marc, and I all piled into Joe's station wagon. Grandma loaded us up with bags of oranges to take back for Mom and Dad. And Marc had to carry the box of gas pump glasses, the gift from the bank. At least she didn't make us take the leftover pot roast.

We were surprised to see some of the people we'd been with at the pool waving to us as we pulled away. They called to us to have a safe trip and, most surprising, to invite us back. I guess they had as much fun as we did this afternoon. But Ted didn't even show up to say good-bye.

Lisa and Paul and their grandparents followed behind us. I wished Paul was sitting next to me.

The airport was as busy as it had been when we'd arrived, except that all the people were either suntanned or red and peeling. Some of the people almost looked happy to see their children and grandchildren leaving. They sort of pushed the kids out of the cars when they stopped at the terminal. And some grandparents zoomed off in their cars, leaving their families on the sidewalk. A lot of people were struggling with net bags of oranges. In fact, the main smell in the airport was oranges—plus some leather smells from luggage.

As we pulled up to the entranceway, I saw a familiar shape: a man with his arm extended and finger pointing toward the parking area. His sharp voice boomed, "You can't park here." But the man who barked the order was smiling. It was Ted, and he stood proudly in his uniform. We obeyed Ted's directions and wished him good luck as we pulled up further to park.

"Have a good trip," Ted called after us. "I hope you come back at Easter," he added.

Inside the terminal I heard a grandfather say, "Next year maybe we could meet the grandchildren at the airport, give them their presents, and put them on the next plane back."

Another grandmother said, "You know I love the

sound of the PITTER-PATTER of little feet . . . going home."

I was glad to hear at least one set of grandparents say that children's voices were like a breath of fresh air. But I was even happier when *our* grandma and grandpa hugged us tightly, not wanting to let go. "We'll miss you, Stacy," Grandma said. "We'll telephone and visit that way. If you have something special to tell us you call and reverse the charges, you hear?"

"Okay," I said. I didn't want to let go, either. I hugged back so tightly, Grandma said "Ouch," and laughed.

Then she kissed Marc and said to Grandpa, "We could fly up North now and then, too, with our Senior Citizen discount." She looked at me. "We sure miss your mom and dad. Kiss them for us, a million kisses."

"A million kisses?" Marc groaned. "Yuk!"

Then Grandpa said, "We're not glued down here. Who knows? After a few months of Sundays we might want to open a little shoe store—or move back to Brooklyn for half the year. Maybe we could trade apartments with someone who'd like to try out Florida for size before they retire."

"The page is empty. It's for us to fill it," Grandma said.

"Listen to her," Grandpa interrupted. "A regular philosopher, your grandma." Then he turned back to Marc and me and said, "And you'll soon see. Lemon Cove will be a place for you to visit and enjoy." He winked at Grandma.

I kissed Grandpa and said, "We'd enjoy being with you anywhere."

I kissed Grandma and said, "When you go on Wednesday, say hello to the people at the Center for me."

"Okay," Grandma promised. "And don't lose the present." She pointed to my pocket. "Open the envelope on the plane and put it in a safe place." She cleared her throat and I could tell she was holding back tears. I was, too.

Then Reggie and Joe and I hugged and kissed. They gave us their grandchildren's address. "I wish they'd come down at Easter," Joe said.

Lisa and Paul's grandparents kissed us all good-bye, too.

The boarding announcement blared in the background. Everyone in the airport seemed to be wishing each other a Happy New Year. There was a lot of hugging and kissing everyone else one more time between "did-ja's," like "did-ja take your tennis racket?" or "did-ja remember your toothbrush?"

"With all the hugging and bags of oranges," I said laughing, "someone's gonna end up with orange juice." I handed our bag to Marc and stopped to take one last look as my group walked ahead.

That's when I was most surprised of all, because suddenly, in this crowd of people, I was whirled around and a voice said, "I guess all this kissing is catching. I just gotta do this while we're alone." And then I was being kissed. Not by Grandma, Grandpa, Reggie, or Joe. They were way ahead with Marc and Lisa and their grandparents. It was a real kiss—a Paul kiss. It was quick, but I could feel the braces on his teeth.

"Wow!" I said to myself, filled with joy and relief that my braces didn't get stuck to Paul's or make sparks, the way people tease.

"Just to say hello, and Happy New Year," Paul whispered. "We'll be home before midnight." We boarded the plane and took seats next to each other. "I like you, Stace," Paul said. "I couldn't wait another minute to tell you. We'll be with Lisa again and she's got a big mouth and big ears and eyes."

"I like you, too," I said and I think I may have turned "embarrassed red" once again. But it wouldn't have mattered. It would have just matched the color of Paul's face.

As the plane soared north we talked about how great things had worked out. And once during the flight when Lisa and Marc had gone to the "lavatory," as a bathroom on an airplane is called, Paul put his arm around my shoulder, and for a minute we didn't say a word.

I felt like I'd grown during this vacation, even though this afternoon my swim team bathing suit had fit exactly the same as before. I figured I'd rather be like Joe and Reggie and Grandma and Grandpa and keep on changing and growing up . . . forever.

On the airplane, after the snack of what tasted like plastic cheese sandwiches, Paul and I exchanged phone numbers and wrote on the two stamped post-cards that I had left over. Then we compared schools. At Paul's school in Morristown they call junior high middle school, and you go there for sixth, seventh, and

eighth grades. Our swim teams both have good coaches. We talked about the movies we like, too. Both of us like happy endings. I never figured out exactly when I started to like Paul or when he started liking me. I guess when you're ready, you're ready!

---

Dear Grandma and Grandpa, Reggie and Joe and all our Florida friends,

Thanks for a wonderful vacation. And special thanks to Grandma and Grandpa for our last Chanukah present. Marc and I were so happy when we opened the envelope and saw the airplane tickets for our Florida Easter vacation.

Love,
Stacy (& Marc & Lisa & Paul)

P.S. We're sending a postcard to Reggie and Joe's grandchildren inviting them to join us Easter vacation at the improved Lemon Cove Condominium. We sure hope they can come. Lisa and Paul will try to be back, if they can.

P.P.S. For some reason the plane trip home to New Jersey will be fifteen minutes faster than going to Florida. I think it must be a tail wind from so many of the grandparents waving good-bye!

---